Bishop & First Lady Pimpin In The Pulpit

Author Tray Real

Published by Author Tray Real, 2023.

BISHOP & FIRST LADY

Pimping In The Pulpit

Copyrights © 2023 Author Tray Real

This is a work of fiction. Similarities to real people, places, or events are entirely coincidental.

BISHOP & FIRST LADY PIMPIN IN THE PULPIT

First edition. September 27, 2023.

Copyright © 2023 Author Tray Real.

ISBN: 979-8223858461

Written by Author Tray Real.

Synopsis

B

eing blessed with a spiritual and prophetic gift is a gift from God, not from a Theologian School. I was born to parents who made an ominous choice to pimp me out in the name of God, verses rearing me according to the word of God. This caused me to question his existence along with my own.

The Bishop and his she devil First Lady were my pimps and my abusers along with my parents and others. They used and manipulated scripture to validate their actions. They were known to pass the plate more than they fed the parishioners a good word.

I met Marco at school and found that we had a lot in common. Our families also attended the same church. After we began spending time together, I thought that I loved him. I soon discovered that my love differed from Websters.

Eventually, I declared liberty over my life. Remembering that I serve a God who gets down in the pain and struggle with me. I learned through my trials that God was in this fight I considered my life with me. Therefore, pain could not have the final say.

Attorney Body and I became one another's anchors. She stayed the course and prayed me through. Although what she revealed about her and Marcos's connection would have had me running toward the heal, she stayed the course until she became a choice.

God placed me in this position. Although I felt overwhelmed, and consumed with negativity and doubt at times, I was the right person for this job. My calling was bigger than what I was able to see with my worldly vision.

With all that was done to me by those who claimed to love me, God would not allow me to die. I had to learn not to let doubt drag me down into the darkness that was trying to blind me. Fear could no longer supersede my faith, nor could I confine God to any specific religion.

There is a new devil on every level, and I am now armed and equipped, having no fear. This fight is not mine. With that being said, Father, this is your fight! I'll be over here standing on your word!!!

Prologue

"M

r. and Mrs. Ricks we are doing everything in our power to save Kenna and the baby," Dr. Jones began. "We put her in a medically induced coma to reduce the work of her brain cells and to protect them from increased pressure inside of her skull. With prayer and patience, we should see some improvement, but for right now, it is a waiting process," Dr. Jones stated.

My mother sat in a delusional shock as my father lost control.

"BABY!? Dr. Jones, my daughter, is only sixteen years old! She is a straight "A" student heading off to a top Theological College to pursue ministry next year! Not to mention, she is one of seven students in the state expecting to graduate Cum Laude at the age of seventeen with honors of distinction! This must be some type of a freakin' joke!" my father yelled.

Doctor Jones had no sympathy for my parents. It was obvious Dr. Jones was livid. I was not expecting him to chastise my father, but he did, "As a matter of fact, it's not a joke Mr. Ricks! She is in a medically induced coma to save her freaking life sir! She has pressure built up in her head, or did you bypass the fact that I even mentioned that small detail? She will remain in MICU until we are able to get her vitals down to normal and see brain progress. She has been raped a multitude of times, SIR! If I were you, and I am not, I'd be trying to figure out who raped and beat my child, as well as reach out to the nearest Police Department! Oh, here's one, maybe I will do the honors because evidently you and the misses haven't had enough common sense to! It's either that or call your clergy and a coroner, she won't make it another year going through the abuse she has endured!" Those were the last words spoken before Dr. Jones got up and stormed out of the room.

I felt the tension in the room around my parents. My mother who never stood up to my father in my presence, finally stood up a little too late and said, "My child better make it you slithering heathen! I cannot believe that you are sitting here in denial of what was obvious to us both. I promise you that you and those other Judas will burn in hell, and I am going to make sure I help you get there before I do!" she spewed with hatred.

My father did not say anything immediately. My mother must have tried leaving the room because I heard my father say, "Where in the hell do you think you are going, and to whom do you think you are talking? I am still the man and the head of this family! I will rat your behind out for your part in this entire fiasco before I take all the blame for any of this mess!" he said with heat and venom.

My mother yelled, "LET GO OF MY ARM!"

The next thing I heard was my father screaming, "STOP WOMAN! OUCH!" My mother was lighting him up with a barrage of punches.

She then said through gritted teeth, "It's over, I will meet you in HELL!"

I heard mother moving around. She moved in the direction of the door. Just as she opened the door, a nurse was at the door and asked was everything okay. I could hear the conversation and interaction, but I could not respond. I heard the cries, anger, and disappointment, but there was no empathy left in me for either parent. I heard the police identify who they were, as they interjected into the discussion. The police made the announcement that they were there with warrants.

I could hear an officer say, "Mr. and Mrs. Ricks, you are both under arrest for child abuse, participating in a prostitution ring, neglect, racketeering..." and numerous other charges he read. The list of charges went on and on. I could not believe that my parents both were involved from the beginning, but then again, I could. "You have the right to remain silent. Anything you say can and will be held against you. You have the right to an attorney, and if you are unable to afford one, one will be appointed," the police officer said as he read them their rights. I could hear my mother's cries and my father's denial of participation.

It was finally over! I can work on healing. *Thank you, God, you can allow me to wake up now. God, can you hear me? I do not have to die. I can go back now they cannot hurt me anymore.* I laid in peace and thought about everything leading up to all of this, and how alone I felt.

I lived in a lonely world. One of abuse, molestation, and no one to talk to about any of it. My parents kept me purposely secluded from others, so that I could be easily influenced and manipulated by them and not question my situation. It is considered control, not love. I was always made to feel like things were my fault. My feelings were swept under the carpet as my heart became numb. I doubted the God that the church wanted me to believe in. The pulpit was Satan's playground. It was filled with a bunch of lowlife gangsters, prospects, and suspects. I witnessed who they were with their bibles and robes, as well as who they were with their spikes and horns. I knew the evil they possessed. I lived in that turmoil and named it life. As I lay in this bed fighting for the only life I knew, I have so many unanswered questions and loveless emotions.

I can only imagine how those hypocritical church folks are going to spin this story. Only time will tell, as it unfolds the truths and untruths that will linger from the lips of the sinners." God, if you are listening, I need to run this by you as I lay here in thought. *Father, some may sympathize with my truth, and some may not. Either way, it is a truth I had to endure, and I really do not have any right or wrong answers. I only have questions and doubts. My story is one of many, you should know, you wrote it. I will be judged regardless. I am not ashamed of who I am, I am ashamed of how love treated me.*

I should try praying for forgiveness over all who have come up against me, and those who will judge me. I go back and forth with this because of the rocky foundation I grew from. I am trying to understand why you chose me for this assignment God, because I am just a kid. It's not meant for me to understand because you're still working it out. In the meantime, can I wake up? I am beginning to overthink everything, and I am ready to get up out of here.

I heard alarms going off. CODE BLUE! CODE BLUE! I could hear people rushing around giving orders. What is going on now, I began thinking. I was being hooked up to some type of machine, I can feel it. Someone extraordinarily strong began giving me chest compressions and counting. There was a ZAP!

"Hey, ouch that hurts."

"One more time," I heard Doctor Jones say. That same process was repeated again.

"Ouch, stop that crap hurts," I thought.

"We have a light heartbeat, let's get her stabilized. I will need to insert a tube down her windpipe. She needs help breathing, FIGHT KENNA FIGHT!!" Doctor Jones shouted hysterically.

I can't be dying; this can't be it. I cried on the inside. Maybe it's best that I die in this life, so that I can be born again. I can be reincarnated into someone anyone can love. This way I can express my interpretation of love to others. At least the abuse would be over. There would be no one else to disappoint. Reflecting back on my life, I never would have dreamt things would be this way. I was always taught that God protects fools and children, so where was my protection? Was this primitive thinking or biblical prophecy? Maybe if I think back on my life a little harder, I will understand why my life was filled with so much abuse, turmoil, and pain. It may also explain why I am laying here pregnant with the Bishops baby.

My Earliest Memories

I was always a great student. I enjoyed learning and my teachers were super nice. Sixth grade is almost over. We had a few weeks left in the month, a lot of testing and extracurricular activities. It was a Friday afternoon, and I had not been feeling well. Mother prayed over me, gave me a banana, and sent me off to school. I was not sure if I had to do the number two or throw up, but I knew I was sick.

"Mr. Farmer, may I go to the restroom please, I am not feeling well," I asked.

"Yes, you may," he began. "Please take the hall pass off of the hook," he said.

I took the hall pass and ran all the way to the restroom. I made it just in time. I felt weak and began sweating, not understanding what was going on with me. It felt like I had to do the number two, so I lined the toilet seat with toilet paper and almost went into shock. I was bleeding! Oh, my gawd, how did I do that? I'm dying, I thought, before a substitute teacher, Ms. P, heard me crying as she walked past the restrooms.

I could hear her walk in and say, "Hello, hello," as she walked past the three stalls against the walls. I was in the third one. "Are you okay sweetie? What's wrong?" she asked in a sweet angelic voice.

I cried and tried to explain, "I have a belly ache, I have thrown up so much that it made me bleed."

"Oh honey," she said. "You've started your menstruation."

I continued crying but stopped long enough to ask her, "What is menstruation?"

Ms. P went on to explain to me what was going on with my body. My mother never talked to me about this type of stuff, therefore I had no clue. I was scared, and Ms. P could tell. She asked me to hold tight as she ran to the office nurse and retrieved a sanitary napkin. She instructed me on what I needed to do, as she stood outside of the restroom until I was finished. She then guided me to the nurse's office where the school nurse allowed me to lay down with a heating pad for a few minutes before returning to class.

Mr. Farmer was very understanding. He assured me that he'd be there for me if I had any questions or needed help. I thanked him and took my seat in the back. The end of the day bell rang, and we were released to go home. I had no real friends outside of a kid that would speak to me periodically named Marco from the church. He was very shy, and so was I. His family was very influential in the community and gave a lot of money to our church. We would sometimes eat lunch at the same table and never say a word. A few times he asked if I was going to bible study or a program just to have a conversation.

As I began my journey home, I had no idea that Marco was behind me until I heard him say, "Hey."

I turned and said, "Hello." I turned back around and kept walking. I was nervously excited. He had grown so much in the last few years. He reminded me of a gentle giant. I knew that I was not allowed to be seen speaking with him or any other boy. My father would whip me for sure. I heard Marco say something under his breath. Yet, he did not say it loud enough for me to hear what he mumbled. I turned to ask him was he talking to me and saw three guys from the school laughing and horse playing around behind him. They even went as far as to push him to the ground and laugh, as they ran across the street screaming "bloody marry." I had no idea what they were talking about, nor did I care. I helped Marco get up off the ground. He brushed him self-off and said, "Thank you!" Marco handed me his sweat jacket and told me to tie it around my waist. I looked at him with questioning eyes. Before I could ask why, he said, "You have blood all over the back of your pants." It dawned on me that I had started my period. I still wore the same thin sanitary napkin I had on from earlier. I tossed his jacket back and took off running and crying. I was humiliated!

I arrived home to my dad and the Bishop sitting in our living area. I ran right past them into my room. I was so embarrassed and upset not knowing what to do, that all I could do was lay there and cry.

"Kenna!" I heard my dad yell. Fuck him, I thought. "Kenna!" again he yelled. I did not budge. I could hear my father telling my mother how I ran past without acknowledging him or the Bishop. He ordered her to get me out of my room immediately.

Mother threw my door open and grabbed me by my arm. She tried jerking me out of the bed but was met with resistance. She raised her hand to smack me as I looked at her with hatred, as if to say, "I wish you would!" It is her fault that I had no idea what menstruation was. I am humiliated! She realized at this point that I had blood on my rearend. As if this entire situation was not enough embarrassment for a lifetime, she screamed for my dad to come to my room.

He entered my room, looked at me as she pointed to my bloody rear, shook his head, and chuckled before saying, "You are impure." As he left my doorway, he instructed my mother to get me up and make my fishy tale take a bath. Most people would think "wow, poor thing!" Nope, not my parents. My father paraded himself back in the living room and told the Bishop that I had started my menstrual. He also made sure that he mentioned I had blood all over my fishy little self, and I had better get up and clean myself and my linen. They both laughed like it was the biggest joke ever told.

My father instructed my mother to go purchase me a package of sanitary napkins and hygiene wash. He also instructed her to be back within thirty minutes with a receipt and his change. He and the Bishop laughed and talked more in a whisper after she left.

I sat in the tub and just relaxed before I heard the door open. I figured it was my mother returning, so I did not open my eyes right away. I felt someone rub on my breast, and it startled me, so I jumped. It was the Bishop. He smiled, pulled out his private part, used the restroom and left back out.

This was the first time the Bishop touched me, but not the last. Each year up until the tenth grade it grew worse. He allowed his wife to partake as well when I was promoted into the tenth grade. They would both periodically make statements about my body being stacked, or that I was maturing. Which was sick! They were both predators. This was also the year they began pimping me out and the beatings got worse. I often wondered why I did not tell any adult, a teacher, counselor, or the police. It finally dawned on me why. I was petrified! The Bishop knew everyone. I was not sure to whom he was connected. My parents were involved somehow, the school never brought me in nor asked me one time. It seems unbelievable, but it is true. I was sheltered with little knowledge of life outside of the church world. I had no family, or close friends. Only Marco. Let me fast forward.

Chapter Two

Changing
Four Years Later

E

xcuse my French, but I am tired of the Bishop and his funky wife, First Lady. She always smelled of "White Diamonds." It smelled horrible with her skin chemistry. She would do things to me separate from him. Never together at this point. I do not like women, nor have I ever been attracted to one. She would make me do things to her that were totally disgusting. If I didn't want to or resisted her, she would smack and punch me around, he'd just force me.

His penis was a turn off! My immaturity and childlike ways were evident. This was not something I was prepared for nor enjoyed. I was a child who had never even seen a naked body outside of my own. Let alone a married grown man. Bishop would pinch and pull on it, in order to make it stretch, white stuff would be coming out of it. It was disgusting to me. I would bleed because the little ugly thing would poke me too hard. He had the nerve to get mad at me when I didn't want it in my mouth. He would smack me and force my mouth on the thing. I thought about killing them both, along with a couple of those old faithful Deacons.

I planned to sit and try talking to my mother about what was going on. I know she has seen the bruises, black eyes, and noticed my behavior change. My grades had even began slipping a little. My parents would always try to validate everything with scripture. Their favorite scripture was from Proverbs 13:24 that read, *He who spares the rod hates his son, but he who loves him is diligent to discipline him.* For the life of me, no one can convince me that the God I grew up serving gave anyone permission to use a rod to beat another person. If nothing else opened my parents' eyes up to what I was going through, the beatings should have. They ignored the black eyes and the bruises if they were not adding to them. Mother would sometimes bring me ice, but that was it. I bought Tylenol on my own. Neither questioned the Bishop nor First Lady as to why they were beating me, or if it were them who was guilty.

My father would still go to his Deacon meetings and meet with the Bishop on a regular basis. The other Deacons who joined in during the week, stayed away from me in church on Sundays. They wouldn't even look in my direction. The only Deacon who never attempted to touch me in a bad way was Marco's father. I never said a word to him, nor did he treat me any different. I knew in my heart though that he knew or assumed something was going on. Bishop had the Deacons pass the plate after he received another revelation and spoke in tongue. People were searching for change because the plate was passed so many times. I was happy to run up out of there, only to be sent back later for my lesson.

It was a Tuesday night and time for Bible study again. I arrived a little late because I secretly joined an African American spiritual group. I lied to my parents and told them that I joined a young Christian Leadership group. I knew if I told them the truth, that they would forbid me to stay. The Bishop had my mother brainwashed into believing that I was being paid by the church for helping with Bible study. In my heart, both of my parents knew what was going on. Maybe not extinct, but they knew it was something. The Bishop and First Lady would line up parishioners' females and males, normally at least two a night, and make me have sex with them. It did not matter whether it was oral or penetration, as long as they were paid. Once I arrived, I did what I had to do, and left to go home and scrub my body.

Bishop and First Lady were perverts of the worst kind, and my parents were money hungry uncaring animals themselves. My mother's hand was out as much as my father's when I arrived home. I am shocked that he did not pimp her out for the money. During this same period, Marco and I began speaking a little more. I wanted to confide in him, but I was scared that he would tell his parents, and they would say something to the Bishop or my parents. Worst scenario, they would make him stay away from me. I had a lightweight crush on him. He finally asked me out on a date, and I told him I would have to ask my parents.

Marco was always such a gentleman. He would be fuming when I showed up at school or anywhere bruised up. He was very suspicious of my parents and always stared my father down as if he wanted just a little proof so that he could beat him down.

I was scared to ask them to allow me to go on a date with Marco, but I was going to do it anyway. I prayed about it the best I could. Although my life was horrible, I still tried praying and having a little faith. I knew either way it went, at some point, I'd be judged by my parents for even bringing the idea up. Mother was scared to go against my cheating no good father, so in order to keep him happy, she would judge and put me down along with him.

In the beginning, when I would complain about going with the Bishop or First Lady because they were strange, I'd hear them both say, "Judgement is one of the main commandments you shouldn't violate." They would then get with some of their prayer warrior friends over a shot of scotch and talk about the other church folk, recite scripture, not understanding the context of what they recited. This happened frequently. I would stay in my room and talk to God myself and ask questions. I'd lay still and listen for a directive or answers. I could never understand why people played with God. I'm speaking in reference to ministers, Bishops, pastors or simply people of the cloth. I'd be sitting around just listening sometimes and hear some of the elderly say, *"Follow the word and not the man, man is human and will error."*

My thinking was when they get ordained into ministry, or take an oath, aren't they held to a different standard or are all sins the same? Shouldn't they be held with higher accountability? The bigger question is, how can you follow the word of a man or woman that are so heaven bound until they are no earthly good? Especially if you know or think that they are misleading because their actions do not match up with the word they preach and claim as God's word.

Issues of this nature are being swept up under the holy cloth and drizzled with a little holy water from Jerusalem. The standard answer given is "God is in control." It is rare that anyone tries removing these pimps and money hungry vultures. Replacing them with true God fearing and anointed Ministers of the cloth. Some have periodically been exposed on television after they have spent half of the church's building funds on yachts, homes, cars, clothing, and other material gain. Isn't that considered embezzlement? Fraudulent appropriation of money or property for one's own use in the name of God? I guess just like with all things, there are always bad apples in a bushel. Maybe Judgement day will be the day that they will pay for their sinful ways. Because the scripture I read in Mathew 7:21 said, *Not everyone that saith Lord, Lord shall enter the kingdom of heaven.*

I may be getting off subject, but when you have gone through what I have continually gone through, it makes you compare what you have been taught, and your life experience against reality. I have more questions than answers, and I am sick of hearing the same old handed down excuses. As a young adult, I have experienced how politicized churches have become. In my opinion they have become an Organization. Everything has become money motivated and not faith based. People are going to church, but do not have church on their mind. It feels like we are reversing back into the year of two hundred A.D. that I've also studied about. This was a time in history when the first compilation of the established texts resembling what we refer to as the New Testament came into agreement. What people do not realize is, giving is choice based. Although in Leviticus, Numbers and Deuteronomy it states, that the tithing system was organized in an approximate seven-year span. If I am not mistaken, this was to support the Levites within the gates and to assist the poor. In the bible, there is no scripture that outright says you must tithe on money you receive as a gift; this doesn't mean that you can't. Tithing is basically a decision between you and your God. If the Bishop had it his way, we would have a clothing tithe, a jewelry tithe, a Bishop need a new watch, new car, new prostitute, new scotch, and the list goes on tithe.

What happened to genuine love-based choices? What happened to giving and helping the less fortunate without string attachments? Some churches do, mines don't. We don't have a food pantry, clothing pantry or any kind of help for the community. They don't even visit the sick and shut in, nor do they make hospital visits. The focus of my church is on the Bishop and his she devil. The Deacons didn't even hold them accountable. This included my own parents. All my parents, and some of the other Deacons were good at doing was passing the collection plate. "Let me take you back to where I went through the fire, and how after thinking about all of this, I know that the God I serve and love, saved my soul.

Chapter Three

The Devil Had Game

I begged my parents not to force me to continue going to church Tuesday through Sunday. I also pleaded with them to allow me to have a normal childhood life. "The Bishop and his wife are...," I began with my complaint. My father stood up and smacked me in my face. My mother sat sternly watching.

"Do not speak ill of the first family in our home, do you understand me?" my dad said in anger. This was his normal reaction toward anything I did, or anything he felt was challenging his authority. At every angle, the answers were no. I had no social life with kids my age. My life consisted of studying to stay in the top of my class, and worshipping. Tuesday through Saturday I was pimped out and a sex slave to the Bishop and First Lady, the perverted child molesters. Sundays were bidding days for the male parishioners and a few female parishioners after church. As far as I was concerned, they were real prostitutes. My parents believed in the Bishop and First Lady more than they believed in me. I guess this is what you would call "birds of a feather flock together." Let me delve back into the Bishop and his she devil.

It was a Monday evening. I was in the kitchen helping my mother prepare supper before my father arrived. She wanted to try a new recipe out of her recipe book seeing that my father always complained about her cooking. My mother is Hispanic, and her first name is Camilla. My father's name is Paul, and he is African American. Father grew up eating soul food and mother grew up eating Tortilla's and Tajadas. I enjoyed the best of both worlds. Mother and I were enjoying our girlie time together for once. So, I thought it would be a perfect time to bring the topic back up about the Bishop and First Lady. I wanted to tell her about some of the parishioners, as well. I also planned to ask her to speak with Father about me seeing Marcos from school. I knew it was a lot at one time, but it was worth a shot. I had to do both. I owed it to Marco to ask about the date, and I owed it to myself to expose the Bishop and his workers. Marcos was a very bright and fun guy when he was open to talk. He was my peaceful place. I was not scared of anything when I was around him. We continued to eat lunch together periodically at school. He was one of the only students who would even speak to me. I knew he liked me; I could sense it and I liked him.

"Mother may I ask you a question?" I began. Mother looked at me a little uneasy before saying,

"Please do not ask me anything that is going to anger your father. You know we do not keep secrets around here," she stated. Well, that pissed me off! She does not keep secrets, but he does. I know for a fact that Mr. Deacon Ricks, my father, has a whole girlfriend and a possible baby. We will get to that later.

"Forget it," I said as I walked off to go set the table. My mother and father took walking off as a sign of disrespect. I was expected to ask to be excused and I did not. Mother walked up on me from behind and pulled my locks and asked me had I lost my mind?

"Your father will be walking through those doors any minute now. Get your act together before I help you young lady," she stated. I was highly pissed and cared less if either parent knew it. Just as she let go of my locks, my father walked in looking exhausted. "Hello dear," my mother greeted my father as he walked in and sat at the table. He reaped of day-old vagina. Mother must have gotten a whiff too, because she turned her nose up and marched off into the kitchen before, he replied.

Being funny, I asked, "How was your day father?" He never answered me back. I did notice a scratch on his right cheek that looked fresh, so I snickered. This did not sit well with father, so he ignored me as well. Mother came out of the kitchen with a new attitude and his plate. I asked to be excused and went into the kitchen to fix my mothers and my plate. When I came back to the table, I caught the tail end of him saying, "...not another word!" I gave mother her plate and took my seat.

"Father, how did bible study go tonight, or did you have to bypass due to work?" I attempted again to engage in conversation.

"Bible study went pretty well. We are starting a mentoring program that I signed you up for. We decided to also have counseling sessions for marriages, Christian dating, and abuse training for a small donation," he stated. He has to be kidding. I was unsure whether to laugh or continue with my questions. I thought this would be a perfect opportunity to ask him the question I was going to ask mother.

"Father," I began. "What do you feel would be a proper age for me to date? Seeing that Christian dating will be part of the new counseling session. I would love to get married and have a Godly family with children like you and mother." I stated.

My father looked at me like I had asked the devil to serve us dessert. He chewed his food and just stared at me. Before I knew it, he threw his plate at the wall and said, "That's your damn problem, you want to rush to be a whore just like your mother!" My face dropped. A whore like my mother, wow I thought, coming from the man who has his only daughter being pimped out by the Bishop. I didn't say another word. My mother's head dropped as well. He then ordered my mother to go and fix him a Scotch on the rocks. Mother jumped up and headed to their makeshift bar in the living room. She hurried to fix her Deacon husband a drink so that he would stop whining. Welp, I guess I won't bring up the Bishop or First Lady. Me and mother both might get a beating.

Father stood, looked back at me, and said, "Don't worry about dating right now. Get your grades together and get right with the Lord." He walked off like he had just gave me the best advice in the world. I asked to be excused in order to complete my lesson, study my nightly devotional, and to have my own time with God.

After I returned to my room, studied, and completed my lesson, it was time for my nightly prayer and devotional. I needed to ask God again for a clear understanding. I went into my secret place which happened to be my closet. I felt safe in my closet from the world and the mass confusion of the world.

Heavenly father, I come to you with a heavy heart. I need your guidance; your protection and I need clear understanding. I am not being taught properly father. What I am experiencing, and learning cannot be your way. Your teachings and words cannot be this cruel. Father, I am listening, so please teach me to understand your word with discernment. I am being taught and exposed to loveless ways, and abusive behavior. My parents swear that they are Christians and live Godly, yet they are also a part of turning the pulpit into a business and not a sanctuary. Father, you see all things, yet I suffer abuse, rape, and being traumatized almost daily. My parents want me to live one way, and they judge and live another. I know people who fear reading the bible father because they are confused as to what to believe, just as I am. Bishop teaches us that your word is prophetic. You spoke your words to prophets who wrote the prophetic message on scrolls. Yet, the way that they interpret your word brings me pain, not love, hate with no forgiveness to give.

I joined another ministry to help me in my understanding. So, I come to you asking for discernment of the word in order to understand my purpose. I have to go back to the beginning of religion and allow you to speak to me and through me. I have no trust in man nor woman. Especially since I am learning that some of the messages you prophesied to different prophets were not even included in the Cannon or bible as we say. Church was designed to develop the people in every way, mentally, physically, and in every other aspect, and I do not see that being done. God you are not a God of confusion, so why am I confused? Man excluded your messages due to several varied reasons from non-belief by the counsel, to political reasonings during their time. Some of the books were plagiarized, and opinions of the all-male counsel were feminist. You do not represent those things, so what am I to study? How do I pray to you? Am I not receiving your answers because I am a girl, and you do not speak to women prophetically? I was taught that Magdalene was a prostitute and that you did not give her prophecy. This being the reason her book was not included in the Cannon. Why would anyone vote to keep your word out of the bible if your word is truth, it's a living word, am I right?

How am I supposed to live my life by your word father if I have no clear understanding of what your word is. I know you exist. I just do not personally feel that your words are confined to what is written. Please help me to understand and protect me on my journey. I am a lost sheep. I love you, Father. Amen.

After I prayed, I came out of my closet and prepared to lay in my bed and study. I felt that once I prayed, I would receive a revelation to help me understand. I decided to read Romans 14:8 in my King James version of the bible. I soon drifted off to sleep. I awoke to my alarm going off.

I got up, showered, and dressed to prepare for a long day. I had school and I also had to go over to the church for the mentoring program my Father signed me up for. I ran into Marcos right before lunch and promised to meet him outside for lunch. It was a little warm today, so I decided that we would find a nice tree to sit up under and just enjoy chatting it up. I was excited to see him.

Marcos and I met up and found a beautiful Eastern White Pine Tree to have lunch under. We caught up on each other's lives and what we had planned for the rest of the week. Marcos stated that he was grounded because he couldn't recite scriptures when he was quizzed by his parents. He got a couple of scriptures incorrect, and this caused him to be punished. His parents were as strict as mine. He was able to go to work and back home to study. He also said that his parents wanted him to attend the mentoring program a couple of days a week at the church, so maybe we could see each other then.

Lunch was over and it was time to head back in. We cleaned our trash and headed toward the door until I heard someone call my name. It was Bishop and First Lady. I excused myself and told Marcos that I would see him back in school. Marco's stood and watched for a few minutes. I watched the Bishop and First Lady glance in his directions several times during their impromptu pop-up meeting with me.

I briskly walked over and greeted the Bishop and First Lady. The look they gave me was odd and very peculiar. I watched as they both looked from me to Marco and back. First Lady began with, "Hello Kenna, you look beautiful today. We look forward to you attending our new mentoring ministry, which will be separate from our little bible sessions," she stated.

I began thinking, I know good and well they didn't come all the way up to this school to say that. These two are up to something. "Thank you, and I am looking forward to this new ministry. My father spoke highly of it last night at supper," I lied and responded.

I caught Bishop licking his lips and looking at me sideways, as First Lady looked from me to him smiling. These two are strange, I said to myself. First Lady turned on her pivot and said, "I can hardly wait. Come along dear." Bishop began walking to his car door as I began walking off because now, I am late getting back from lunch.

"Oh Kenna, it is not a good look seeing you eating lunch with a boy alone. I am sure Deacon would not take kindly to that. Watch yourself, even at school you are representing the Lord," Bishop said before driving off. Here we go with the extortion. I bet you nine times out of ten one of those two weirdoes' are going to mention seeing me to my father and all hell is going to break loose or use it over my head. They think they are slick. They are here recruiting other young naïve kids. I am on to them.

Chapter Four

Abusing A Child Of God

I arrived at the church about fifteen minutes early. I wanted to be prepared and just relax a little before everyone showed up. Bishop was walking through the sanctuary and saw me enter. I figured that he was in the sanctuary preparing a message with some substance, but that was a joke. He's a hustler that robs, and hustle people in the name of Jesus. No one challenges anything that he does. They allow his unaccountability. Although he wears the title Bishop, and claims he attended a top Theologian school, school makes students. It takes God to make a preacher.

He made it his business to come and greet me. This time it was different. He gave me a hug and pushed himself into me like he wanted me to feel his privates. Previously, he would wait until we were in his office. Now he was getting bold. I was extremely uncomfortable. I am sure he could tell because he released me after I tried prying myself loose. We walked back into his office where his wife sat looking over some paperwork. I greeted her and took a seat.

"What's wrong dear," First Lady asked. Before I could say a word, Bishop got up and closed the door.

"Nothing much," I responded.

"Well, you look like you are tense, or upset. Let me help ease some of your tension," she stated.

First Lady got up and came over and began rubbing my shoulders. The Bishop watched on and I could tell it was exciting him by the smirk he wore. Previously, it would be one or the other. Never both of them at one time. I began feeling nervous and trying to think of ways to get out of there. First Lady acted as though she accidentally touched my breast. I knew it was on purpose, so I said, "Thank you, but I am fine now."

Bishop began walking toward us and sat down on his desk directly in front of me. "Come here," he demanded. I got up, but not fast enough because the next thing I knew, the Bishop grabbed me by my locks. "I have permission from your parents to train you up, and you will do what we say. Is that clear?" I was petrified at this point. I agreed as he again pulled me into him to hug me. This time he gripped my butt and pulled me in between his legs. He began grinding around on me. I started crying, I was a wreck! First Lady gave me a napkin and said that I would be fine.

It must have felt good to him, because he started going faster as First Lady began touching my breast. I tried pulling away from him, but she smacked me and told me to relax. Bishop unzipped his pants and pulled out his penis. He told me to touch it. I was hesitant and was tired of them doing this to me. It felt weird and nasty. First Lady assisted him in pulling my underwear down. She began touching me down there.

I tried to buy some time in order to think of a way out by saying, "The others are probably waiting."

Bishop was so caught up in trying to stick his penis in me, that he did not hear a word I said. After several attempts he was able to get it in and began pumping me real fast. First Lady began sucking on my breast. I was in so much pain, I wanted to scream. This is rape. It was over as fast as it began. Bishop grabbed me by my throat and said, "If you say a word to anyone, you will die and so will your parents. Get dressed and get your fast tail out of my face."

First Lady got me a wash rag and took me to the Bishop's personal bathroom to assist me with washing up. I had blood running down my leg. I was so upset that I could not stop crying.

"Shut your mouth up and clean your face. You only have two more tonight before you can leave," she said. I was so mad and hurt that I wanted to fight her.

She left and locked the door behind herself. *Lord why? Please answer me, please!!* I am sick of this! In walked the assistant Bishop.

"What's wrong he asked?" I just sat in the chair with nothing to say. "Come here, the cat must have your tongue." I continued sitting where I was. He is just going to have to kill me, I am tired! When I did not answer, He took out his cell phone and called Bishop. He told Bishop that he wanted his money back because I refused him service or tell the secretary to send him a new one.

Bishop barged in his office, grabbed me by my throat and said, "Thy shall obey thy master! You cannot grow in understanding of the Lords heart and desire for our lives if you do not obey! Now obey and do not make me come back in here!" The Bishop walked right back out the door, his assistant then turned the locks.

The assistant Bishop looked over at me, and then said, "Let's try this again, come here!" I got up and started walking towards him just as all of the power went out. It was very dark in the office. I could see him looking around like it was a hoax.

Someone began knocking on the door and asking in a sweet voice, "Is someone in there?"

I headed to the door, and the assistant Bishop grabbed me covering my mouth with his hand. He tried to swing my body in the opposite direction, but his weight wouldn't allow him to. I broke free as he fell backward against something, I unlocked the door, and ran. The entire church block was pitch black. I ran out and kept running until I was almost home.

"Where do you think you are going young lady?" the voice asked. I looked up and it was First Lady.

"Home," I responded.

First Lady then ordered me to get in the car. I kept walking. She then said, "If I get out of this car, I am going to kick your tale."

I prayed and kept walking. First Lady pulled her car to the side and parked. I sped up my walk because I knew I only had a block and a half to go and could run if need be. She walked up on me and grabbed me by my hair. She threw me to the ground and started hitting me as I balled up on the ground. "*God protect me, God, I need you,*" is all I kept saying.

The next thing I knew, First Lady was on the ground being pummeled by a guy in a mask that was built like Marco. She never seen him coming and did not see him leave after he kicked her in her face and knocked her out. He took off and ran in the opposite direction as I left her lying there and skipped the rest of the way home.

I walked in the house after brushing myself off. Both of my parents were sitting at the dinner table acting strange. I acknowledged both and neither ever looked in my direction. I went to the kitchen to fix myself a plate, and there was nothing but a spoon full of Tuna Casserole left. I put it on a plate with two slices of bread, poured a glass of water and went back to the table. Once I scooted myself up to the table, I heard familiar voices coming from our living area. I just listened to the male chatter and never turned around. They were not sitting there when I first walked in, where were they...?

"Do not ignore our house guest Kenna! We have raised you better than that. Take your behind in there and acknowledge the Bishop and the Assistant Bishop. They were kind enough to make sure that you made it home safely after the lights went out," my father stated.

"Hello," I said and kept eating the little food I had. My father knocked my plate to the floor, breaking the dish and knocking over my water. In my head I began thinking about how childish he was. I bent down and picked up the broken pieces as well as the food, put it all in the trash and headed to my room excusing myself.

I heard the front door close minutes later. I began thanking God they left. I picked out some pajama's and headed to my bathroom to shower and get ready for bed. It felt so good to allow that hot water to hit my body. I was ecstatic that First Lady had gotten knocked out. As I smiled for the first time and scrubbed myself, I wondered if it was

Marco who had done it. I got out, dried off, and brushed my teeth. I headed back out of the bathroom and into my bedroom. I stopped mid stride when I saw the Bishop and his assistant in my room. The Bishop sat on my vanity stool while his assistant laid under my covers in my bed. My parents left and left me here with these two devils, I could not believe it but then again, I could.

"Where are my parents?" I asked.

"They left to go check on my wife, the First Lady, after you attacked her and left her for dead. Get your ass in that bed and make my money before I beat you half to death," the Bishop demanded.

"Father, please do not leave me hanging. I rebuke you Satan in the name of the father, the son, and the holy spirit. Father protect and cover me. Amen.

I slowly walked in the direction of my bed and sat down. The assistant grabbed me and began touching my body. I wanted to throw up but knew they would make me clean it up. The Bishop sat watching and instructed his assistant to pull the covers down on the bed so that he could see my body, and he did just that. He made me pull my gown off in order to take in my body. I froze and couldn't do it. My eye's watered because I was scared.

God, please help me, please, I prayed!

The Bishop got up and closed fist hit me in the face. "When I tell you to do something you do it!" he shouted.

I began crying out loud. "I am tired of this, just kill me I shouted! Kill me, I cannot keep going through this!" I spoke.

"Shut up before someone hears you!" the Bishop ordered.

The assistant hadn't said a word. He had a blank emotionless look plastered on his face. Finally, he broke his silence and said, "Look man, she can just give me a blow job. I don't have time for any of this."

"You heard the man, get to sucking."

I hurriedly did what I was told. Once I was done, I jumped up and locked myself in the bathroom. The two men talked in a whisper for a few minutes and then left out. I listened by the door to make sure that I heard nothing. I brushed my teeth, gargled, and went back in my room closing my door and cried myself to sleep.

Holy Thou Are Not

I wanted to sleep in, but my alarm clock said get up. I got up but could hardly see. I went into my bathroom to wash my face and brush my teeth. When I looked in the mirror, I could not believe how swollen my eye and the side of my face was. I cannot go to school like this I thought. What am I going to do? I decided to put on a little foundation to cover up the black and purple bruising but could not do anything about the swelling. I parted my hair on the side and swooped some of it to hide my eye. It worked for the most part. I grabbed my book bag and headed out of the door. I did not want my parents to see me with make-up on.

As I walked out, I noticed a car driving extremely fast down our street and swerving up into our driveway. This caught my attention. I stood behind a tree and watched as a young woman jumped out of her car with a little child. She stormed up to the door and began hitting the door pretty hard. My mother opened the door from what I could see, and the lady rambled off something. Next, I witnessed my dad burst out the same door and grab the ladies arm. She began hitting him and kicking him until he hauled off and smacked her. What did he do that for, because the lady put her child in her car, popped the trunk and started fighting my dad some more. She was beating him up and talking junk. Finally, I watched as she hauled off and kicked my dad between his legs as hard as she could. He dropped to his knees screaming for the Gods. My mother tried to help my father up but couldn't do much between his rolling around and the lady pushing her away. Finally, those two began fighting and my mom lost big time. After the lady beat up both of my parents, she went back to her car, got the child out of the car, pulled a suitcase out of the trunk, and left the child alone with both of my parents and peeled out.

I laughed almost all the way to school. I was so happy that I almost completely forgot about my face. Marco was walking toward me saying something and all I could do was smile.

"Hey happy lady," Marco said as he continued walking closer. Once Marco was close enough to see I had on makeup and my face was swollen. His smile quickly changed into a frown. He grabbed my face gently, pushed my hair out of my eye and stormed off.

"Wait Marco, wait!" I called out. I ran over to him and quickly said, "I am okay. Please stop worrying about me." His eyes were watered. I knew he was angry. I didn't see him anymore that day. I searched for him that day and for several days after. He was nowhere to be found.

After school I arrived home to a house full of tension and a little boy playing and running around in the house. My mom wasn't speaking, and my dad looked as though he was about to have a nervous breakdown.

"Hey little fella, what's your name?" I asked him knowing darn well who he was.

"My name is Paul," he said.

"Well, hello Paul. My name is Kenna. Nice to meet you," I said.

He said, "Catch." He threw the ball so hard that he knocked over the lamp, and he took off running and laughing. I picked up the lamp and said goodbye to Paul Jr. Yes, junior, he is my brother. My father and mother both stopped and looked at me.

My father said, "Kenna darling, where are you heading?" My mother stood still waiting for my reply as well.

"I have bible study and the mentoring program tonight," I said.

Both of my parents in unison said, "You should stay home a few days and relax."

Forget them, let them stay here with this child and bond, I thought. Kenna darling, gag me! I said to myself.

"I wish I could stay home a few days, but we are discussing Lady Magdalene and I was interested in learning more about her and why she was considered a prostitute," I responded. They looked at one another like two silly people would as I walked off thanking God for showing up once again.

I entered my room to put my things away and noticed the little boys things were in my room. That wasn't going to work, I thought. But then again, maybe it will. Let me continue praying about all of this and not jump the gun. I left back out of my room, said my goodbye's, and headed toward the door.

My father said, "Kenna, I can drop you off and pick you up if you'd like."

"No, I am good," I began. "I can walk, thanks." I opened the door and walked out.

As I walked down the street in the direction of the church, I thought I saw Marco, but it wasn't him. Several days have come and gone. Finally, I saw him coming out of the neighborhood hardware store. I began jogging in order to catch up to him. I didn't want him to see me and then run off. I got behind him and tapped him on his shoulders. It scared the crap out of him. We both snickered a little before we spoke.

"Where have you been Marco?" I asked with my hands upon my hip.

"Hello Kenna, I've been around," he said. He looked a little sad as he began walking slowly back down the street. "Kenna, may I ask you a serious question?" he asked. I thought about it before I answered back.

"Sure, go ahead," I said.

"I don't know what's going on, or why you are being abused, but..."

"Stop Marco, you don't have to say anymore. There is a lot going on that I have never told anyone about, you are right. The situation is bigger than me. I was always scared to say anything to you or anyone in fear of you saying something to your parents or somehow getting back to mine and the church," I confessed.

"Kenna, I would never do such a thing to you. What we have ever said amongst one another, even us sneaking and seeing one another, I have never spoke of."

"Thank you, Marco, I appreciate you! Can we talk later? I am on my way over to the church. Aren't you coming?" I asked him. At first, he did not respond. Marco seemed like he was always in some type of deep thought.

"No, I am not coming to sit up in there with those hypocrites. I would consider myself just as bad as them."

Maybe he is right. It would be just my luck that if I do not go, one of the perverts would find me and kill me. I would be lying somewhere dead, I thought. "Let's talk through email when I get in tonight," I said. Marco agreed and crossed the street before we neared the church parking lot.

When I walked through the side door of the Church and entered into the sanctuary, I saw the Bishop doing something that I have never seen him do before. He had four young girls between the ages of fourteen and fifteen sitting on the pews giving them some type of instruction. They were visibly shaken up. The Bishop looked over at me, and never once acknowledged anything about me standing there listening. I was appalled at the things he said to them. What he said to them were the same things he has said to me in the beginning. I took a seat behind the girls. They never even glanced in my direction.

"Yvonne," the Bishop began. "Go into my office and wait on me, you know the routine. To the rest of you, Bishop want's a new Cadillac, so you all will be working a little extra seeing that the First Lady is continuing to rest and heal. The rooms are set up, don't disappoint me. Your dismissed!"

Each girl scurried away with fear on their faces. I sat with my arms crossed and mad that I had never had the courage to stand up to the Bishop, First Lady, my parents, or any of my other abusers. Today those young ladies gave me the courage to fight back, and I am going to stand my ground.

Bishop sat on the edge of the altar just looking at me. I began talking to God...

Father, I need you! I believe that all things are possible through you. Now I understand that sometimes you give your hardest battles to your strongest soldiers. You don't call on the equipped, you equip the called in good works. You chose me father according to your purpose for me. I believe in you and have faith that you are right here with me. So, Father, let's do this! Amen. I stared back at him with no fear. I've learned in my studies that fear is a sin. My father God said, *"I will provide for you. For it is he who will fight for me."* Bishop's face began looking strange, like he was in pain. He broke out in a sweat and began holding his chest. I continued sitting there for a second longer. I stood up just as Bishop reached his other hand out asking me to help him.

"I've been in God's way long enough Bishop. Go to him, he has the final say." After I said that, I walked off and dialed 911. I reported the molestation at the church and said, if they would hurry, they could catch them in the act.

I went into Bishops office to retrieve the client list of names he would refer to. He normally kept the list in his middle drawer. Also, on the list were the days, and amounts charged and paid per sexual act. Bishop created another list since he had been recruiting with our names, how much we made and the days he worked us.

That was quick I thought. I walked out of the Bishops office and into the sanctuary. The police were running up in there like SWAT. I pointed in the direction of the rooms and walked out of the building. It hadn't dawned on me that Bishop was gone until I began walking home. I didn't stick around because I didn't want anyone asking me questions.

The streets were dark, and the night was chilly. I walked home Thanking God for giving me understanding in what I had misunderstood. My focus was redirected off of what others wanted me to believe, into a more powerful place. The spiritual connection that I yearned for, the Godly discernment I asked for. I began feeling how thankful I was to know and understand that God's timing was always on time. My focus was rerouted into a more powerful place, my gift of understanding.

I felt someone's hands cover my mouth. I began getting lightheaded and dizzy. I knew it had to be First Lady; I smelled the White Diamond on her skin. She tried dragging me to her car, but I fought back. Although I was dizzy, I still had most of my bearings. She swung on me, and I swung back and kept swinging. I flipped her to the ground and began punching her in her head. I heard Bishop scream, "Get off of my wife you whore," before he kicked me in my head and began beating me with what felt like a metal bar. The last thing I remembered before I was out was a big person in the shape of Marco stabbing the Bishop and hitting the First Lady across the head with the pipe that Bishop had hit me with. We both must have blacked out.

Chapter Six

God Led The Way

I could hear crying and panic, but I couldn't wake up. It was my mother, and I heard my father, They fussed amongst each other before the doctor came to speak back with them. Doctor Jones began explaining about some surgery they had performed on me. He also explained that they put me in a medically induced coma. Doctor Jones was furious with my Father's statements and lack of concern.

Both of my parents were chastised by Doctor Jones as he stormed out. Soon I heard the police come and arrest my parents on several charges of which they were definitely guilty.

The most amazing thing followed. I began talking to God and feeling a sigh of relief. I felt free and no longer feared the loveless life into which I was born. Yet, I wasn't able to awaken. *God I can return now.* I began saying. I wasn't returned right away.

I began feeling a strong presence. I wasn't sure who it was. I wondered if it was Marco. Did Bishop and First Lady make it or are they back for revenge?

"Kenna, I love you and always have. I have never forsaken you, nor will I ever. It is true that I give the toughest battles to my strongest soldiers. I never abandoned you through your pain. You found strength through me to continue. My love for you, my child could never separate us. When you began shifting your thoughts, trusting in my timing, and having patience, you were able to see that the battle you tried fighting on your own was mine. False teaching was among you, and many followed. Because of them the way of truth was blasphemed. In their greed they exploited others with a false word. Do not believe every spirit but test the spirits to see whether they are from me. Many will come in sheep's clothing but inside they are ravenous wolves. Condemnation will be their end and will correspond to their deed."

I hear you God. Thank you, Father!

I felt so at peace, like a big burden had been lifted off of me. I smiled internally knowing that God was with me, and that I wasn't forsaken.

"Kenna, can you hear me? If you can, squeeze my hand," I heard Doctor Jones say.

I not only began squeezing his hand, but I opened my eyes for the first time. My vision was a little blurry at first, but it cleared up enough for me to see Doctor Jones, a nurse, and Marco and his parents. Marco came over and stood next to my bed and grabbed my hand lightly. I looked up at him and smiled. I was happy to see him and shocked that he was there with his parents.

"How do you feel Kenna?" Doctor Jones asked.

"I feel good," I responded with slurred speech.

"That's great!" he responded as he checked my vitals. Once the doctor checked me over, he explained that someone would be coming to get me to do an ultrasound, and a special scan on my head within the hour. I thanked him as he smiled and exited my room.

Marco still stood next to me. I said hello to his parents as they stood at the foot of my bed. They both came around closer to the side and told me how sorry they were for all that I had gone through. I said, "Thank you," as they excused themselves to get a bite to eat.

Marco just stood holding my hand and smiling. "Uhm," I began. "Are you going to fill me in, or do I have to wait until I am released to get the four-one-one," I said smiling.

"Sorry," he began. "Your parents are still in jail. The little boy's mother got him. She pressed abandonment charges, and child neglect charges against your parents, on top of all the other charges they are fighting. Bishop and his she devil stayed in the hospital for a few days with police guards. They were transported straight to jail once they were deemed able to leave. The Assistant Bishop, the Deacons, along with the female parishioners who abused you were all arrested. They had more charges than I could list. When the police ran up in the church and caught those members in the act with the young girls, the members sang like a bird along with the young girls. Seems like this has been going on for years. No bail was allowed for your parents, or the Bishop and First Lady. The community has been outraged! Kenna this situation has gone worldwide. It has reached every news channel, social media, and newspaper," Marco said.

"Wow," I thought. "Marco, tell me something," I said. He squeezed a little harder and just looked at me. "Was that you both times?" I asked. Marco just looked at me and smiled. That was admittance enough.

"What are your parents thoughts?" I asked him.

"My parents were totally shocked! My dad said if he would have had an inkling any of that was going on, he would have turned the church in himself. He wants his tithing money back. He feels like they spent it on supporting their illegal activities versus taking care of the church and the expenses of the church. He hasn't made me pick up a bible since," Marco stated.

"Well, I need you to bring your bible up here and study with me," I said.

He smiled at me and responded, "Okay."

Marco's parents returned just as we finished talking, and so did transportation. It was time for me to get my head scan. Marco and his parents promised that they would come every day to check on me. I genuinely appreciated their support and thanked them from the bottom of my heart.

I was transported down to do my ultrasound and then some new type of head scan and taken back to my room. I had time to just lay in peace and think about all that has happened in a new light. I also began thanking God for a new chance and new direction. The nurse came in my room and inserted more pain meds in my IV. Soon I drifted off into a comfortable sleep.

I was awakened by an aide taking blood and checking my vitals. I was hungry and asked what time breakfast was. The nurse put in my order, and I dozed back off until I heard Marco's voice. He arrived bright and early.

"Good Morning'" he said.

"Good Morning, Marco. Why aren't you in school sir?" I asked.

Marco looked at me strange and then asked, "Do you realize how long you've been in the hospital Kenna?" I really hadn't a clue now that he asked. "School is out for the Summer," Marco stated.

"Oh wow," I said out loud.

We sat around and talked about nothing in particular, laughed and really got to know one another. Marco would never turn on the television in fear of me having to relive what I had gone through. He shocked me when he pulled his bible from his book bag. We prayed for a clear understanding before we began to read. We also did something different and interesting for us. We did research on some of the original beliefs. We began with the Traditional African religions, which were animistic in nature. We looked into a little Hinduism, the original Christianity that differs from what we are being taught today as well as the Islamic religion.

In each we discovered that the bottom line for the Creator is love, forgiveness, and humbleness. You can call it whatever religion you'd like, in our opinion. We both decided that we would prefer to be considered spiritual versus being labeled anything else.

Doctor Jones entered my room with my test results. He asked if it was okay if Marco remained, or if I wanted him to wait in the waiting area. I smiled and said, "It's okay." Doctor Jones went on to say that I was healing up rather good. Everything was checking out okay. The only concern they had was that the baby was underweight.

"I do not want a baby, a rape baby at that!" I began yelling. "How am I going to go to school my final year of High School pregnant? I have to figure out how to take care of me let alone a baby. Where are we supposed to live?" I asked no one in particular. "God, not this again. I thought this was over." I said out loud not thinking.

I then heard God's voice as plain as day, *"I have not left you. Trust in me and have faith in my word. As a mother comforts her child, so will I comfort you. Do not worry. Train up this child in the way he should go, and when he is old, he will not depart from it."*

"I'm sorry for the outburst. What do I need to do Doctor Jones in order to save my baby?" I asked. Marco smiled again. Doctor Jones explained that he was putting me on a special diet. I needed more nutrients. He also started me on a prenatal vitamin.

"Kenna," Doctor Jones began. "I contacted social service to help you with housing placement. I wasn't..."

"There is no need for that," Marco's mother and father walked in and spoke. "We are taking her to our home where she and the baby will be cared for. We owe her that much." Marco hugged his parents, and they hugged him back. I was so happy that I didn't know what to say. I thanked God and cried happy tears

Chapter Seven

New Life

I was released from the hospital. Marco and his parents rented a truck and helped me move my things from my parents' home into their guest home. Although it was considered living with them, I had my own little house with two bedrooms, a kitchen, living area and a full and half bath. I was excited! Marco parents helped me move my parents furnishings and my bed over. They bought me dishes, comforters, towels, toiletries, and food. I took all the food from my parents' home also that was of any good. They won't be needing it. I also went in my parents room and opened up their safe. They had no idea I knew they had one. My father had fifty thousand dollars in cash in it and their life insurance. I was the beneficiary, so I needed to keep the policies. I kept the money also. I figured that the little boy's mother would drain their bank accounts with her lawsuits and child support.

I was settling into my new spot and received a knock on the door. It was Marco's mom. "Hello Mrs. Singfield," I said as I greeted her at the door.

She smiled an angelic smile and said, "Hello dear, may I enter?" she asked.

"You sure may," I responded as I moved out of her way.

"How do you like the place so far?" she asked.

"I love the place and the peace," I responded jokingly.

"Kenna, I would like for us to get to know one another better and form a bond. If you need anything, please ask dear. We only ask that you and Marco be respectful of our house rules and don't keep late hours."

"I understand," I began responding.

"School is especially important," Mrs. Singfield continued.

"Make sure when school is back in, you study your school lesson and keep tidy. We grocery shop on Saturday mornings and it would be a joy for me and you to spend that girlie time together." She finally took a breath and paused, as I smiled and agreed with her. She is such a beautiful lady, I thought. "Oh sweetheart, the delivery guys will be here in a few hours to deliver the stackable wash machine and dryer," Mrs. Singfield added.

I wasn't sure if she had more to say, so I smiled and shook my head in agreement. Finally, she stood up and walked over to the door. "Thank you all again so much for welcoming me into your home Mrs. Singfield. I want to sit and talk with the family about everything that has transpired soon. I am unsure of what direction to take next," I stated.

"Yes, sweetheart I understand. Just don't force yourself to bring back such awful memories. Some things were meant to be forgotten. Relax my dear, we can talk tomorrow, get comfy," she responded. I gave her a big tight hug, and she hugged me back. It felt so good to receive a hug. My intuition felt it wasn't genuine this time.

A few hours had passed. I received another knock at the door. It was the Lowe's delivery guy's just like she promised. They delivered a stackable wash machine and dryer set. They not only delivered it, but the workers hooked it up, and got it going for me. She never mentioned that she was having a rocking chair, and a baby bed with all the fixings delivered as well. I was very much appreciative.

The next morning, I was up early and dressed. Marco called to inform me that breakfast would be served at eight. I began walking toward the main house taking in the view. This was a beautiful well-maintained home. I knocked at the door and wasn't surprised that Marco answered it. He escorted me to the breakfast area where everyone sat and ate together. We had prayer and were served an extravagant breakfast. I was starving and prayed that I kept my manners while eating. I didn't want to appear ill-mannered. Marco's dad, Mr.

Singfield, started off the morning conversation. He informed me that he had Mrs. Singfield made me a prenatal doctor's appointment with a new Obstetrician. He also hired an attorney to represent and defend me in the rape case against the church as well as my parents.

He asked if I'd ever thought about being emancipated? That was the furthest thought from my mind at the time. I had no idea what it was, nor what it consisted of. He explained that I was old enough to be emancipated. Which would mean that I would be considered an adult. I was also welcomed to continue living in the guest house until I decided if I wanted to attend college or get a job. The catch was he and her would raise my baby while I pursued my journey. Or I could allow them to adopt the child and they would take care of all of my expenses, and I would have a home.

"Thank you all again! I am profoundly grateful that God has put us all together. I don't know what to do to be honest. I am trying to figure this all out myself, especially since I had no real direction growing up. With the verbal abuse, the beatings, the rapes, and lack of socialization, life is challenging for me right now for the most part. I was so sheltered without a loving relationship with either of my parents, to the point of it feeling creepy! I had no life outside of church and school. I prayed for love and the understanding of love because I have no idea. It can't be anything like what I've been taught and lived. The love I experienced was painful. With the help of God and God's love, I know I will finally experience the true meaning. As much as I do not want to be a parent this young, especially due to rape, God gifted me with this baby in order to learn to love someone unconditionally, outside of myself. I will learn patience, humbleness, and a lot more on this journey. "Marco, thank you for always being my friend," I said as I wiped my tears, and thank you Mr. and Mrs. Singfield.

Marco and his parents got up one at a time and gave me a big hug. After we all hugged, we spoke more on the case with the church. I went more into detail about the Bishop, First Lady, the Assistant Bishop, and some of the Deacons as well as parishioners. We sat around in the living area as I told of how everything began and the things I was made to do played out. Marco's family listened intently to each word. I felt comfortable speaking with them because they didn't pressure me to remember more. We prayed together about our journey going forward and swore to stick together. Marco's parents stood and announced that they had an errand to run. They stated they'd be gone for a few hours, so Marco and I decided to go out back and lay by the pool. We both had on shorts and t- shirts and drank our strawberry lemonade. It was so peaceful.

"I hate that all of this has happened to you. I never told you my truth because I couldn't take burdening you with anything more, so I carried the pain with me. I almost lost it witnessing some of what you were enduring, with no way of helping you. I came home one day and just broke down and told my parents they were losing their child because of their religious practices. I was beginning to hate going to church and studying in the manner in which I was forced to learn or be punished. One evening, I stormed out and walked the streets waiting to run into you. I knew your routine and route. When I saw First Lady attack you the first time, I blacked out. I thought I killed her. I came home more withdrawn and more troubled than before. Another instance, when you came to school with make-up on and your face was swollen, I made up my mind that day that I was going to kill them all. That's the day you saw me coming out of the hardware store. I bought things I thought I would need to get the job done. Every day it got worse for me. I knew then that I loved you."

"Love me?" I said as I looked at Marco. I smiled and reached for his hand to allow him to finish.

"Yes, love you, Kenna. The night the Bishop hit you with that pole, my intent was to kill them both. That is why it was so easy for me to stab him and beat her. I called for an ambulance as I ran from the scene. I ran home and fell to the floor. I began crying out to God for forgiveness. I needed him to protect you, and not me. I begged God to let Bishop and First Lady die. My Father and mother came in the room and saw all of the blood on me. I had to tell them what I did and some of what was going on from my perspective. I had no idea that things were much worse. I asked my parents to listen without judging me. That day sparked a day in my life as well. My parents promised to collaborate with me and to help save you. I confessed how much I cared about you and how much joy you brought into my life. Once the story hit the news and the community, my parents have been right by my side. They have been incredibly supportive and attentive. I thought that they would run once they overheard the doctor state that you were pregnant. They both said that we would make it through this with God's blessing."

"Wow Marco, I wasn't the only one struggling. Thank you for opening up to me. And Marco..."

"Yes," he answered.

"I have loved you since the fourth grade. Remember when you gave me your jacket to hide my bloody pants." We both laughed and continued sitting there enjoying the outside, peace, and serenity.

Marco's parents returned after a few hours. We went back inside to sit and chat with them. I asked them if it were okay to start a family bible study. I enjoyed it when Marco and I did research. I thought it was fun and educational to learn more about different spiritual beliefs. I enjoyed comparing what was passed down generationally as fact, to proof in researched facts of today. It is truly helping to ground me in my spiritual growth. Marco's parents thought that it was an excellent idea. We had our bibles and laptops out. We used the laptops to research religious history in the beginning. We decided to post three questions regarding a religious topic, we then researched the topics origin. Marco's parents were having just as much fun as we were having. It is interesting to research the things we were taught to be true but were unsure of. We delved into Egypt Rome and religions of Ethiopia. The

Reed Sea verses the Red Sea. We went on for hours promising to take it a step further each time. I was getting tired and hungry.

I decided that I would leave. I wanted to go and fix a couple of sandwiches, eat some fruit, and take a nap. Marco asked me to call him when I awoke if I wanted company. "Sure will, I responded." I gave them all a hug and went back to my modest home I was beginning to adore.

Marco's parents came and knocked at my door. It startled me at first until I looked out to see who it was. I opened the door and stepped to the side to let them in.

"Sorry to bother you Kenna, but the attorney called. We need to go to her office within the hour. It seems as though the pretrial dates for your parents, the Bishop and First Lady have been pushed up. The attorney has two days to prepare herself and brief her partners."

"Okay, sure what time should we leave," I asked.

"Can you be ready in fifteen minutes?" they asked.

"I sure can. I will put my shoes on and be right over," I stated.

They left right out, so I put my shoes on, grabbed my key's and purse, and headed over. They waited for me at their door. We all loaded up and drove over to the attorney's office praying that we arrived on time. The traffic was heavy, and the rain was beginning to come down. You could tell that everyone in the car was in deep thought.

We had finally made it. We were five minutes late, but we made it.

"Hello, everyone, my name is Attorney Bracy Body. Welcome," she began. "Let us all introduce ourselves, so that we can get this show on the road," she stated.

We all introduced ourselves to her. She began with giving us the information that she had acquired. "All parties except for your mother, and Deacon Ladson had plead not guilty," she explained. "Documentation was sent overnight to my office marked "Evidence." It contained one page. The page consisted of a list of clients, fee's charged, and fee's collected."

"Miss Kenna, have you ever heard of or seen such a list?" she asked.

"Actually, yes, I have. The night I called the police from the sanctuary, the other girls were in the process of being raped. Before the police arrived, Bishop was having a tough time breathing. I ran out of the sanctuary and into his office to find proof of what was going on. I wasn't looking for anything specific. I just wanted some type of proof. I saw him insert them into his middle drawer on a few occasions, I took a chance and looked. I saw them and took them. I must have dropped them when First Lady attacked me.

"Can you look at this list and see if it is the same list or if this is some scam list that I may need to disregard?"

"Sure." I looked at the list and it was definitely the list. But there is a page missing," I said.

"A page missing?" Attorney Body said more as a question than a statement.

"Yes, there were two papers folded together. The page missing contained more details. Such as initials of people who were on payroll who were receiving these acts, the sexual act's themselves and the names with the dates of service were included," I stated.

"I see," was her response. Marco's parents never flinched. Marco just shook his head.

"Kenna, can you tell me your story from the beginning. Try not to leave out any details. Don't worry about whether the detail is important or not. I will do that part. Take your time," Attorney Body stated. I started from the beginning and told everything and every detail of which I could think. I just felt like I was missing telling something and couldn't pinpoint what it was.

"Wow, what a story. I am so sorry that you had to experience that," she stated. Attorney Body thanked us for coming in and told us that she would meet us at the courthouse at 9:00 a.m. Wednesday morning, if we wanted to wait in a conference room until pretrial was over. Which would be two days from today. She doesn't advise it in this case, but it's on us.

We left and rode back home in complete silence. I think this entire fiasco has taken a toll on us all. I will be glad when it is over, I thought. We finally arrived back, I was tired and really wasn't up for any company. I told Marco that I was tired and that I was going back to bed. I asked him could he come and wake me up when it was dinner time. He looked sad and smiled before saying, "Yes." I went in and laid across my bed. I continued trying to remember what it was that I was forgetting and ended up drifting off to sleep.

The Truth Exposed

M

arco woke me up as promised, so I walked over for dinner. I could easily cook for myself; I had a lot of food. I also have snacks and drinks. I was really being lazy and enjoying being taken care of for once.

I left and walked the walkway to the main house; I smiled as I saw Marco walking in my direction.

"Hey sleepy head," he said.

"Hello Marco," I replied.

"Are you hungry?" he asked.

"I am starving," I replied.

"Good," he began. "We are having fried chicken, collard greens, macaroni and cheese, deviled eggs, cornbread, a triple chocolate cream cheesecake and a peach cobbler. We will be washing it all down with a little bit of Strawberry Lemonade," he stated. My mouth was watered up just thinking about eating. I playfully pushed him to the side and ran through the front entrance. We both laughed as we entered the eating area and were greeted by his parents.

Neither of us took the time to wash our hands, so Marco directed me into their guest restroom, and he went into his own. I began washing my hands and noticed a pill bottle had either fell off of the counter or someone missed the trash can. I reached down to set it back up on the counter and noticed it was prescribed from a Neuro Behavioral Center. The person it was prescribed to removed or peeled off their name and the bottle was empty. Although the bottle was empty, you could still make out the prescribed medication name. It was for Quetiapine a ninety-day supply which was refillable a couple of days ago. I decided to lay the bottle back down where it was and to exit the restroom. They were all waiting for me to return before dinner was served. We prayed, ate, and talked. At the suggestion of Mr. Singfield, we decided to finish our drinks in the living area.

I couldn't help but think about my little discovery, yet I did not want to cause any issues in the home. This was my first authentic experience and opportunity to be a part of a loving family unit, and I did not want to destroy the moment. We all sipped on our Strawberry lemonade and discussed what we expected to happen going forward with the trial. Mr. Singfield wanted to make sure I had no fear of being called to testifying. Mrs. Singfield asked me had I remembered any more details that would be helpful in my case. They also mentioned something that I had never even thought about. The Bishops attorney may order a DNA test be performed on the baby. If his DNA matches, he has half the rights of the baby whether it was caused by rape or not.

This made me think. I became nervous and began sweating profusely. I couldn't allow him access to my baby. I will fight him tooth and nail for full custody and no visitation, I thought. My vision began to blur. The next thing I knew, I was out like a light.

When I awoke, I was in my place, in bed. Marco sat in my room observing me. His parents sat in the living area not saying a word, just sitting. Once Marco saw that I had awoken, he got up and got down on his knee's on the side of my bed and asked me was I okay.

I responded, "Yes, just really tired for some reason." Marco was obviously worried about me and this baby.

He said, "I will send my parents back to the main house, and I will sleep in this chair or out in the living area. This way I can help you Kenna or be the one to call the paramedics."

"Thank you," I responded, as I drifted back off to sleep.

"Rest my child. Do not be discouraged nor fear. I am with you; I am your God and will uphold you with my righteous hand. I will be with you wherever you go. Through eyes of faith, see me on the path before you."

When I awoke, It was the next day. I didn't feel tired or sick in any way. The first thing I did was begin praying, "Thank you Father for your grace, mercy, and protection. Cover me, Lord. I have faith that your will... will be done.

I laid and looked at Marco sleeping peacefully. I decided to get up, shower and get ready for a beautiful day. Once I showered and put on my dress, I heard Marco moving around in the kitchen, and I smelled food cooking.

"Something smells delicious," I said as I walked out of my room smiling.

"I figured that I would break this kitchen in seeing that you hadn't," he said laughingly.

I took a seat at the small table waiting to be served. Marco fixed my plate and returned with his own.

"Wow Marco, this looks fabulous."

Marco fried fish, made grits, potatoes and onions, cheese eggs, and homemade biscuits. Instead of Strawberry Lemonade, we drank orange juice. When I say the food was amazing, I mean it! He can come cook for me anytime, especially since he washes the dishes too.

"Have you called and checked in with your parents?" I asked him.

"Not really a check in," he began. "Out of respect I do certain things. To answer your question, I called and told them that we were having breakfast over here and that we would catch up with them later," he stated.

"That sounds great," I responded.

"Kenna, Do you remember when I asked you out on a date? Well, you never got back to me. Are you saying no to a brotha?" he asked playfully.

"I would love to go on a date with you Marco," I answered.

"Good, then it's settled. Tomorrow after we leave court, we are going out to eat and we are going to go and catch a movie. How does that sound?" Marco asked.

"It sounds wonderful," I responded.

We sat around most of the afternoon watching Netflix until it dawned on me that Marco has not been to work since I moved in here. I hope he hasn't been fired on my account, I thought. So, I decided to ask, "Marco, why haven't you gone to work since I moved in here?"

He didn't answer immediately. He pretended like he was all into the program when I knew that he wasn't. Something is beginning to feel like it is too good to be true around here. I am learning that my gut feeling is Spirit. I sat and pretended such as he. When he responded, I acted as though I didn't hear a word.

I got up and went into my bathroom. I needed to have a little conversation with God. Something is off and I feel it. I don't want to jump the gun, but something just isn't right.

Dear father, I know you are tired of me, but I don't care. I want to make sure that I stay focused on your word and not the actions of my enemy. Something evil is going on. My discernment picked up on it. My spirit is telling me to begin looking for a new place expeditiously. I have the money from my parents safe in order to pay my rent up, and to eat off of for a good while. I will apply to the state to be emancipated and hire my own attorney. Father, I feel your presence around me. Please redirect me if you see me steering off. You are the pilot, and I am the co-pilot. Amen.

After I washed my hands and returned to the living area, Marco had left. He didn't say bye or anything. He just left. Fine with me, I thought. I stayed in the guest house all day. I bypassed dinner and decided that I would take some time to look for apartments. I need to find an attorney to represent me in the emancipation process as well. Before I do any of that, I planned to look up the prescription name that was on the bottle. I need to see what it was prescribed for, so that I will at least know what I am dealing with. I typed the name Quetiapine into my search bar. I was not surprised: "Common brands: Seroquel XR and Seroquel. Quetiapine is used alone or together with other medications to treat Bipolar disorder {depressive and manic episodes) and schizophrenia.

Quetiapine extended-release tablet is also used together with other antidepressants to treat major depressive disorder. Antipsychotic."

One of them suffers from some type of mental illness. I have to play this cool until I am situated. I decided that I would go along with the program, someone is bound to slip up if they are up to something. God will expose them.

I laid around all day sleeping on and off. I made myself get up and eat some leftovers from Marco's cooking, take a shower, and get ready for bed. We had to be in court tomorrow. I wanted to be well rested and ready. Once I ate, showered, and took something out to wear, I went into my room, had prayer, and began my bible study research. I started with the Wisdom of Solomon and the book of Enoch. I watched Yoruba Spirituality on YouTube and called it a night.

I was awakened around three a.m. The baby was causing me issues, so I began tossing and turning. My back was hurting, and my stomach felt cramped. I laid there hoping and praying the pain would go away. There wasn't any medication that I could take because the Obstetrician hadn't seen me as of yet. Maybe it's the prenatal vitamins. I hadn't used the restroom regularly since I have started taking them. I will get some prune juice in the morning while we are out. In the meantime, I am going to be fine, I thought. I felt someone staring at me. I opened my eyes, and no one was there. It was a strong dark presence. I have little to no time for this. "I rebuke you Satan in the name of the father, the son, and the holy spirit. Flee." And just like that the heaviness was lifted, and so was my pain. I went back to sleep. I did not wake up until my alarm clock went off for me to get up.

Chapter Nine

Let The Truth Set You Free

I got up and got dressed. I ate some scrambled eggs with cheese and some toast just in case we had no time to grab a bite. I also packed a few snacks and a couple of drinks. It was seven thirty and I sat watching the news. I hadn't watched the news previously because I did not want to see what was going on, nor what was being said in the media. I knew what I lived and what I had gone through.

World news was on. I continued watching and witnessed people supporting the Bishop, First Lady, and my parents. I also witnessed how they supported a few of the Deacons in their wrongdoings. They painted a picture of me as a troubled child who came into the ministry forcing myself on different members. They claimed I had the First Lady attacked as well as the Bishop. My Father wrote a statement of how much help he tried getting me for what they thought was a mental illness or an addiction of some sort. I turned the television back off. I was livid to say the least. I was ready for war!

Marco was calling. "Hello and Good Morning Marco," I stated.

"Good Morning, how do you feel?" he asked.

"I feel great. I am up, dressed, and ready for the day," I said.

Marco sounded cheerful and in a good mood. I honestly think it may be him with the mental illness. He tries to cover it up, but he can't help himself.

"We are about ready as well. I think dad is pulling the car around," he said.

I said, "Okay, I am on my way out the door. I will meet you out front." I locked up and headed out the door. I greeted Marco's parents and Marco by their car.

As we headed to the freeway, Marco said, "I want to lead us in prayer today if no one minds." We all were excited for him. This was his first attempt at leading us in a group prayer.

"Father, creator of all things. We understand that you are the Alpha and the Omega. You are timeless and exceed all that our imagination could imagine. We come to you in humbleness asking for your traveling mercy, your security and protection, and most of all your love. I ask this in your name, The Great I am. Amun!"

"I am so proud of you Marco!"

Marco smiled all the way to the courthouse. He was just as proud of himself as we were for him having the courage to lead. This was a big step for him. We arrived at the courthouse and were escorted by security up to the third floor, where we met with Attorney Body and her team in a closed off conference area. We spoke for a few minutes before they headed inside the courtroom. News cameras were everywhere, reporters and other stations showed up to record and follow this story. Due to me and the other girls being minors, our names, and faces were not allowed by law to be disclosed. This was only the pretrial hearing where the defense lawyer and the prosecuting attorney meet to discuss the case. Sometimes the prosecuting attorney will try to make an offer to resolve the case without going to trial. I wanted it clear that I was not accepting any of their agreements. Let's take this to trial. I didn't have to be here, I wanted to be here.

As we peeked into the courtroom, there were about fifteen total Lawyers, and Attorneys all sitting around a huge table. Each one walked in like they were not here to play. Attorney Body not only walked that same walk, but by the time it was over, the defending Attorneys ran out with their tales between their legs. Attorney Body and her team did their thing. The next step was to wait for the judge to set the trial dates for the parties involved. I had nothing but time.

Marco was acting a little nervous. I noticed that he couldn't sit still. His parents noticed his odd behavior as well. I rubbed his arm just to let him know that whatever it was, he would be okay. Attorney Body stepped in with her team and closed the door. They explained the next part of this process and how lengthy it could be. She asked did we have any questions before they said their goodbyes and left. We accepted that and got up and left.

We were escorted back to the car and rolled out. It was silent on the way back home until Mr. Singfield asked if we wanted to stop by Bob Evans for breakfast. I was always game to eat. Marco just laid his head back and closed his eyes. There was definitely something going on up there. As we pulled into Denny's Mr. and Mrs. Singfield got out of the car first. I asked them could they give Marco and I a minute. They agreed and walked on to the door.

"Marco, what's bothering you?" I asked as I rubbed his arm. He said nothing. I tried one more time. "Marco, you are the one who said that we were going to do this together, and now you are shutting down on me. You speak to me when you feel like it and shut me out when you don't. Look, I am not here to judge you or watch you go through anything without trying to help. I opened up and allowed you to help me, but you shut down and won't let me in," I stated. A single tear drop came down his handsome face. I wiped it and hugged him.

We just sat there for a few minutes before I heard him ask, "Can we talk later?"

"Sure," I responded. He wiped his face and got himself together. He held my hand as we walked to the door to join his parents.

We were so full of breakfast that on our ride back we all took a nap. Once we arrived, I decided against being anti-social and hung around. Marco needed me. We decided to sit by the pool and drink our pink lemonade and just relax. Marco jumped up all of a sudden and dove in the pool splashing water everywhere.

"Marco, silly why did you not warn me?" I asked in a joking way.

Marco signaled for me to join him. I couldn't because I had on a dress. "I can't get in the pool with my dress on," I said.

Marco smiled his Colgate smile that has melted my heart from day one.

He said, "It's just us, come on."

I got up and jumped in the pool with him. He caught me and held me. This was the first time we had ever been this close. He smelled and felt so good next to my body. But I knew it would be disrespectful to be anything other than a lady with him and in his parents' home. I asked Marco to let me down so that my feet could touch the bottom, and he did.

We both knew that this was dangerous territory. I got out of the water and soon Marco did as well. We both laid silent in our chairs and allowed the sun to dry our clothing. Both in deep thought trying to understand our friendship and the feelings we have for one another.

"What are your plans for the rest of the day Marco?" I asked him.

"Well, he began, today is our date day. So, I still plan to take you out to eat and to the movies," he said as a matter of fact.

I had forgotten all about our date. But I can't let on to him that I did.

"Right answer," I began saying to him. "What time would you like to leave?" I asked.

"The movie starts in a couple of hours. It depends on if you want to eat before or after the movie," he said.

I thought about it for a second and blurted out, "After the movie. I don't want to rush and eat. I want to enjoy our first official date," I replied.

"I had better get up and go start getting myself together," I said to Marco.

Marco laughed and asked, "So early?"

"I want to dress up for you, this is a special day sir," I said as I jumped up and headed through the doors laughing. Marco looked at me and smiled as I pranced off.

I am extremely excited to go out with Marco. I have waited for a while to do so. I decided to pick out a nice dress, curl my hair and pull out my good jewelry. I played some soothing music as I showered and shaved my legs. I decided to paint my nails a soft pink color. I curled and pinned my hair up. I don't wear make-up but decided to wear light lip-gloss. I slipped on an all-white sleeveless maxi dress and jewelry, applied a small amount of Gucci Guilty for women, my all white, red bottom heels and checked myself in the mirror. I looked damn good if I should say so myself.

I heard a knock at the door and knew who it was. I opened the door and Marco stood in the entrance looking like a caramel Adonis. He was a beautiful shy man with a heart of magic. He and I matched up and looked impressive together. He stared at me like he had lost his last breath. His mouth hung wide open like he searched for words that he couldn't possibly form.

"You look like an angel Kenna," Marco said.

"Thank you, Marco," I said. "You are looking very handsome yourself."

Marco stepped in and waited for me to grab my purse and keys. He smiled the entire time showing his deep dimples and pearly whites.

"Stop smiling so hard boy," I said as we both laughed. Marco grabbed my hand as he walked me to his parents car. They gave us permission to drive and said that we needed to be back by eleven.

We arrived at the movies and decided to see a comedy. We found seats after we got our popcorn and drinks. Marco and I laughed and had a wonderful time watching Kevin Hart *Act Up*. After the movie, we decided to go to Longhorn and eat. Marco and I had an impressive time. We spoke about some of everything. I finally found an opportunity to ask him what was wrong with him the other day when he shut down on me. Marco stared at me for what seemed like forever.

Finally, he said, "There are a few things that have been driving me crazy. First, I am on medication and have been diagnosed as Bipolar.

I have been having episodes that are hard for me to control at times. I didn't want you to think differently of me, so I have tried to hide it," he began.

"I knew it Marco," I said.

"How?" he asked.

"You've always been different. That's what I liked about you. I am around you more and notice when you are triggered. I also know that you take medication for it, it's okay. We are a team Marco, I need to know these things," I said.

He looked at me strange and asked, "Did mother tell you?"

"No," I began. "I found your pill bottle on the floor in the bathroom. I never said anything because it doesn't affect how I feel about you."

His face relaxed some, but I could tell he didn't believe me. We finished eating and talking for a while longer. Marco happened to look at the time and saw that it was ten thirty. "It's time for us to go," he announced. Marco asked for the bill and paid it; I left a tip.

On the ride home, I decided to ask Marco why he assumed his mother would tell me such personal information. Marco responded with, "You don't know mother that well. She can be sweet as pie or a vengeful bitch. She is schizophrenic herself." I sat quietly, not knowing what to say.

Chapter Ten

What Happens In The Dark
Is Exposed In The Light

A

fter we arrived back, we said our goodbyes and went our separate ways. I couldn't understand why Marco would say that about his sweet mother. I climbed out of my clothing and took a shower. I decided that I would watch a movie and just relax in my room. I heard commotion coming from the house. I turned my television off and laid quiet as I listened.

"It's your fault mother, just freakin admit it! You were just as involved as the others! I saw you mom, ADMIT IT DAMN IT! I saw you leave out of the back door; I was their mother. I was outside waiting for Kenna to make sure she got home okay. YOU WERE THE SECRETARY, YOU NEW WHAT WAS GOING ON AND NEVER TOLD ME NOR DAD! It was you who helped recruit and put her name on those lists! I SHOULD HAVE KILLED YOU THAT NIGHT TOO!"

"Enough, Enough already!" you two are ridiculous!

I heard a door slam and a car pull off. I knew there was something that I was forgetting! That voice! I need to speak to Attorney Body alone somehow. Tomorrow, I will call myself an Uber and get out of here. I need to get away and think.

I awoke bright and early. I put on a pair of sweats, a t-shirt, and a pair of tennis shoes. I called Marco before he could call me and told him a lie. I explained that I needed to go check on my father's son Paul Jr. I liked the little boy, and he was innocent in this entire fiasco. I mentioned the library and a few more errands. I told him I would be back later. He still sounded asleep and said, "Okay."

The Uber pulled up and I jumped in. I hurriedly asked them to pull out before I was noticed. I called Attorney Body, luckily she had just arrived in her office. I explained that I needed to see her alone as soon as possible. Attorney Body encouraged me to come straight there.

I arrived at Attorney Body's office within fifteen minutes. I began explaining to her everything that I had forgotten. I even told her about the argument in the Singfield home that I had overheard. I explained how it triggered my memory and brought out an important fact that I had subconsciously forgot. I remembered now.

"Thank you Kenna for being so brave," she said. I will look into everything we have just spoken about. I want you to do me a favor though," Attorney Body said. I sat nervously awaiting what she needed me to do. "I need you to get out of that house and go into hiding. The trials may take a year to begin. The process is long and so is the backlog. We are dealing with some powerful people here. Do you have somewhere to go?" Attorney Body asked.

"No, but I will figure it out," I said.

"This is my personal phone number. Buy you a couple of throw-away phones so that you cannot be tracked. I will contact the authorities and do what's necessary on this end. Call me when you get situated," she said.

I rushed back out of Attorney Body's office, went to the library, and got online. I found a beautiful two-bedroom home in North Carolina. It was a two-and-a-half-hour flight. I booked my tickets and checked to make sure I had my money and ID. I was fine. I got everything together just in case something like this happened.

I called an Uber to take me to the airport. I didn't relax until the pilot stated that it was time for take-off. I am going to be fine. I am a soldier; and fear is a sin.

Father, I understand that on every level there is a new devil. I also understand that I am leveling up in understanding. I continue to look to growth and moving myself forward. Moving from one place I call home, into a new place to call home, only means that I am embarking on a new challenge that I know you have equipped and covered me in.

I don't know your plan for my life, nor can I depend on my own intelligence. I can only continue to pray for discernment, understanding and protection. I trust and have faith in your word. Amun

We landed and the first thing I did was find somewhere to sit down and eat. I was starving. While I ate, I got on my phone and googled a hotel that was nearby so that I could check in and relax. I found a Holiday Inn that was beautiful and not awfully expensive, so I called an Uber to take me to check in and paid him a little extra to wait on me. I wanted to hit up Walmart to buy a few things that I would need, and a dollar store to buy snacks and drinks. While there, I bought two throw away phones and headed back. I called Attorney Body and told her where I was and asked her to lock my number in. She mentioned to me that Bishop had bailed out, but his wife was still in jail with the others. I didn't want to hear that but thought oh well. She also said that Mr. Singfield contacted her and said that I was missing. Yet, he hadn't contacted the authorities. She said that she has, and the detectives were finishing up their investigation of my claims. A search warrant along with an arrest warrant should be issued in another day or so. Stay safe and hold tight.

I hung up and gave all of that to God. I refuse to worry. We made it back to the hotel and put all of my items on a dolly. It was easier to transport them to my room this way. Once I put everything away, I decided to take a shower and throw on my new pajama's. I got my fruit and plopped down on the bed. I called the management company of the house I was interested in, just to see if it had been rented out. The agent was a really nice lady to speak with. She assured me that it wasn't rented, and she would be more than happy to show it to me. We set up an appointment for the morning at nine and said our goodbye's. I laid around and read different scriptures. I was getting tired, so I decided to pray and then go to bed early.

Father, Creator of all things from the beginning to the end. My life has been a rollercoaster ride. From being born into a family of evil unloving parents, to being basically sold to a Pimp and his First Lady in the pulpit. I've discovered that church is inside of me. I don't need to be confined within walls to understand your will over my life. These lessons have taught me that unless you prophetically gift a person to minister to the people, going to any Theological School, obtaining every degree under the sun, or sitting in judgement of others, can't and won't make you ordained.

Father, some of these so-called People of the cloth are robbing people blind in your name. What happened to me for the love of money is a notable example. Father, please continue to cover me as I take this spiritual journey. Amun

I awoke the next morning bright and early. I checked to make sure that I had everything I needed before I headed down to the lobby for breakfast while I waited for the Uber. It was a buffet breakfast. I got in line to fix my plate and felt someone behind me tap me on my shoulder. I turned around expecting someone to ask me to pass them a plate or silverware and looked Satan and his accomplice dead square in their eyes... "Bishop, Mrs. Singfield..."

T

he look on my face wasn't one of fear, it was one of shock. Shock was the closest to any emotion that I could gather. I was shocked at how easy it was to be tracked down. I was also somewhat shocked that the Bishop, and the church secretary Mrs. Singfield, had the audacity to unite in order to find me. I wasn't going back into any situation that I was able to escape. I understand that grace is connected to my life. Therefore, I must not allow frustration and anger to take control. I have a new opportunity that is objective of evil doers. Yet, I struggle immensely with anger and confusion. I try praying my way through situations and tend to replay the pain in my head. I've endured pain and abuse longer than I have endured any other emotion. I hope one day I will be able to reflect back and say, "This is my testimony." Until then, I will listen out for the voice of God. As of yet, I haven't heard anything back. But I did pray. I prayed according to my expectations and thanked the Divine Creator in advance. I also took the opportunity to look both demons in their eyes, as I stood ten toes down and rebuked their evil ways away from me. I hope God comes through with some Godly discernment real soon, because I feel some heat coming on, and I am ready to get it popping off up in here!

As I stood in silence, I tried wrapping my thoughts around why either travelled in search of me. Not only that, but once they found me, what did they think would happen? Are these the proper questions to ask or was this picture bigger than my human understanding?

I decided that in order for me to know exactly what they wanted, I should just go ahead and ask them. So, I did just that. "What can I help either of you with?" I asked. Mrs. Singfield looked at me as though she was possessed. Her eyes were empty and dark. There was nothing there. She was hollow and a shell of who she represented. Something is seriously wrong with this lady, I said to myself. I promise, if she tries to grab me, I'm swinging! I will repent later.

"You need to come with us young lady!" Mrs. Singfield demanded. I didn't fear her, actually she was annoying to me.

"You might want to get away from me! You and the rapist Bishop!" I began shouting. Just that fast, I had lost control. I had a flashback of my father and all of the yelling and screaming he would do. "If you are backing him up, you are just as guilty of being a rapist, a molester, an abuser, and pimp as he!" I said sternly and with as much venom as I could spew. "I am not going anywhere with either of you! Actually, I am puzzled as to why you are here, and what gave you the notion that I would willingly leave with you? The last time I checked, the Bishop was awaiting trial and you were home with your family. Which is where you need to go back to!" I yelled.

I disappointed myself. By allowing them to dictate the situation and anger me, not by their words, but by their presence. Darkness was present and in control, and I was unsure of how to get control back.

The Bishop chuckled a little like this was all a game to him. He tugged on the front of his pants, pulling them up on his stomach before saying, "We need you back at home child. The members miss you;

you have a calling on your life that only God could have anointed," he spoke.

I looked at him and shook my head before saying, "I rebuke you Satan!"

He continued on as though no words were muttered by me. As far as he was concerned, I had no voice. I continued listening as he said, "The congregation supports me, just watch the news. They bailed me out and helped us to locate you in order to take you back. You are one of us and I am your Bishop, you will do as I say!" he spewed like the lying snake he was.

The Bishop stood tall as though he had just given the perfect sermon. What neither one realized was the fact that they had just lit a fire under an already ticking time bomb. Before I was able to think about my actions, I took on a negative posture. Without thought, I stepped up to the Bishop and said, "Mr. Bishop I am glad you came." Those were not the words I intended to say, yet they were the words that I released. They both looked at one another and began looking around at the crowd that formed a circle around us. Both bearing smiles of joy, like they had just hit the lottery. All they needed at this time was a collection cup.

I peered in his eyes as I continued, "I have a few things on my chest that I have been wanting to get off for a long time now, and I think it is high time that I do. It's people like you two that make it difficult for people who want to attend a church or place of worship to do so. I used to wonder how people could say that they believe in God, and not organized religion. I didn't understand it because I was young and uninformed. Abuse and lies were what I was taught and suffered at home, and in the church I considered the home of my God. There are many people who seek places of worship and a prophetic word. They yearn for the love of God and seek a church home, synagogue, or a place of worship looking for a prophetic word. They end up encountering people like yourself who sell them false hope, drain them mentally and financially. Based off of opinion and not facts. I consider it misleading the flock. These same people end up like me, lost and confused. There are others in this world who have endured the same mental and physical abuse that had become my way of life. With no voice and no clarity. There are also others like me who have been taken advantage of physically with nowhere nor anyone to talk to. Trapped mentally in a box with no top or bottom. They suffer silently and alone due to embarrassment, or like my parents did me, they were kept isolated from reality."

"Let's not mention the spiritual side of this, where questioning the presence of God becomes a normal conversation piece. Your false prophets stand in the pulpits playing with the word of God and are truly responsible for changing the original words that were prophesied through translation. Words were translated in a way that were beneficial to the religion that it represented. Not you per say, in some cases, but man changed the translations. The church council of Hippo made the choice to include what they believed to be scripture, not what may have actually been scripture. They then allowed the translations from Hebrew and Aramaic into other languages. In the process of translation Mr. Bishop, words were changed to fit the belief. Just like under your leadership, you have taken the word of God and used it in a manner that is beneficial to your beliefs!" I stated with frustration. This fact is part of the reason why people are so confused from the name or names of the Creator God, Allah, Asma, Abdullah, Yahweh, or God's. Or whether we should call the son Jesus, Yahushua, Isa, or another secret name.

"We learn wrong, pass incorrect information on and we teach wrong. I went there to say this, Change your lives! You've ruined so many through false teachings. If you are unsure of what is supposed to be taught and practiced, go to the Creator, and ask for Godly discernment. You both should know this!" I stated.

Mrs. Singfield walked away and sat at the table as though she was preparing to have a meltdown. "Listen you two," I said in a calm and more settled way. "What you all have done to me was horrendous, and I know now that your day is coming. Especially you Bishop and your she devil of a wife, along with my parents and the others. You're just wolves in sheep's clothing. I get it!"

"There is a God who knows your evil ways and have a punishment with your names on it. You care nothing about the hungry and sick parishioners you've denied help to, because they didn't tithe enough. I've witnessed you personally Bishop, take the tithings or offerings and invest in your big home, your multitude of cars, and other material items of value. Don't get me wrong, we all like wonderful things and work hard to possess them. My problem with you and others like you sir, is the fact that you mislead people in order to acquire said things. Isn't there a scripture that reads, 'Do not lay up for yourselves treasures on earth, where moth and rust destroy and where thieves break in and steal. But lay up for yourselves treasures in heaven, where neither moth nor rust destroys and where thieves do not break in and steal?' Or how about the one that says, 'Work hard and become successful in life but don't think of yourself as better than others because of your material wealth. For it is he who gives you the ability to produce wealth.' Does any of that ring a bell?" I asked. There was complete silence. The looks on the Bishop and Mrs. Singfields face began to change. People that were gathered around looked upon me as though I had awakened something in them through my message. I continued to speak my peace and on things I have discovered by researching in this brief period of time away from the church and my family. They both needed to hear this. Maybe while they are locked up, they will think back on some of my words.

"Bishop, you have people convinced that you are prophetically gifted. Things may have started out that way, but once you figured out that you could make just as much money being a pimp, a pedophile, a molester, and the list goes on you..."

The Bishop stopped me. "Hold up young lady," he began. He didn't like the idea that I pointed those facts out, he began adjusting his pants again and fidgeting around. Pulling them up high on his waste and peering around. He had the nerve to be upset. The Bishop stepped up closer and continued. "Look here young Lady," he repeated. "I will not stand here and allow you to speak to me in this manner! Get your stuff and come along so that we can return home! We can discuss your concerns when we get there," he said.

The Bishop made the mistake of telling his secretary to grab my arm and try not to make a scene. Mrs. Singfield reached out to grab me and I pushed her into the Bishop. I was heated! "Don't you ever touch me again," I said! No one tried intervening, everyone just stood around like they were waiting on the next episode of Family Matters.

"This was no joke. I am sick of you bible thumpers, this is my life, and I am tired of all of this! I am too young to have to endure any of this. I will not allow you to ever influence my life again negatively! You are not a Bishop you are a Pedophile who rapes young girls and make them do ungodly things to make money. And for the record Charles, seeing that you barely practice what you preach anyway, from what I am learning half of what you preach is not the way the word was prophesied. You have become so heaven bound until you're no earthly good!" I said as I stepped back.

In my mind I wasn't going anywhere with either of them. They can't make me; I am not the same little girl that I was. Just as I was having a talk with myself about changing my mindset in order to change my walk. Out of nowhere the Bishop belted, "Get your tale over here before I drag you out of those doors!"

I jumped up and stepped in closer to him until our noses almost touched and responded, "I want you to! As a matter of fact, I triple dare either of you to touch me! This is a new day; I will dog walk you back into the pews you fornicate in and beat the holy hypocrite out of your sidekick. Touch me!" I said, now I am pissed again!

I knew that the God within me had me covered, yet trouble kept rearing its ugly head. As I stood waiting for one or the other to make a move, something told me to begin rebuking the thought of doing evil. I really didn't want to sin because they have sinned against me. I wanted to show them that I did not fear them any longer. Fear was a sin alone. I had a personal battle going on inside of my head that I tried shaking off every day. *"Cover me Father, I need your strength to stand firm."* This entire situation made me feel like I was either going crazy or bipolar myself. Satan was not letting up. He tried planting doubt and confusion in my head every day. I am struggling Father. As I continued with the standoff we had going on, I couldn't help but to continually feel as though I was being punished. Am I being punished because I am struggling with forgiving the Bishop, First Lady, my parents and all who have beat, raped, and abused me? Why aren't they being punished? I was the kid who was taken advantage of. This is where I don't get it. In the King James bible, John 1:9 says, *"If we confess our sins, he is faithful and just and will forgive us our sins and purify us from all unrighteousness."* But then Matthew 6:15 says, *"But if you do not forgive others their sins, your Father will not forgive your sins."* I am not in a place of forgiveness just yet. Thoughts were shooting through my already confused and anger filled mind. Just as I finished making that statement, a calming voice began saying,

"My child, you do not have to question my word, nor will you understand this battle because it is not for you, it's mine. Be not afraid or dismayed by reason of this great multitude. Have faith in my word. My word is assurance of things that are hoped for, the conviction of things not seen. Without you having faith in my word, it is impossible for you to please me. I am a rewarder of those who believe and seek me. Trust in me with your heart, not with your understanding. I will not forsake you."

I needed to hear that; it was right on time.

In my calm unbothered faint voice, I turned to the people who stood behind me and asked, "Can one of you please call the police?" I explained quickly. "This man and woman are here to kidnap me and are trying to force me to go with them against my will. He is out of jail on bail for molesting me," I stated. That was all I had to say before I noticed the young lady making the call. Charles was easing his way toward me; I saw him out of the corner of my eye. "GET AWAY FROM ME!" I demanded. Bishop Charles nor Mrs. Singfield expected this type of response from me. They were so used to me being scared and fearing them. They had no other come back for this. I said nothing else. I just stared at him, just as he stared at me. I began praying and rebuking him in silence.

An officer walked briskly over to the Bishop and Mrs. Singfield as other officers pulled in to assist. "*Thank you father,*" I thought to myself. The Bishop tried giving the officers a tough time until they threw him on the floor and roughed him up a little bit.

He began screaming scriptures and telling people to go live in order to post his unlawful arrest. I am quite sure that he's on probation and shouldn't have left the state without permission. The Bishop was led out of the door and read his rights.

Mrs. Singfield muttered, "You will wish you never messed with me, your baby..." she purposely stated low enough for me not to hear the end. She stared down at me without cracking a smile. She was also led away in an awaiting police car and read her rights. An officer came over to speak with me. I was in deep thought about what Marco's mom said. I had no understanding of why she wanted this baby, my baby.

The arresting officer broke my train of thought by asking me to explain what had transpired. I explained that the Bishop and Mrs. Singfield tried to kidnap me. They tried forcing me against my will. I briefly summarized what had taken place, making the officer aware that we had an ongoing legal issue that has not gone to trial yet. Per my attorney, the Bishop was given bail. Yet, I am sure that it came with stipulations. The officer wrote a few things in his report. He then explained that a detective or someone from their office would contact me further for more information. The courts and the proper authorities will be notified in Ohio. Most likely the Bishop and Mrs. Singfield will be expedited back to the state, he informed me. He handed me a piece of paper with the written report number. We then said our goodbye's.

Chapter Twelve

My Faith Walk

I found a small table in the rear and away from everyone. I needed to have a seat, I was mentally exhausted and nauseous. I planned to head back to my room and call an Uber after I relaxed for a moment. Although I was proud of myself, my nerves were all over the place. I needed to pray and get something to eat. Praying should relax my mind and body. One of my discoveries thus far is the feeling I get knowing that I have not been forsaken. I can speak to him and unscramble my thinking in order to correct my thoughts.

Heavenly Father, you knew the Bishop and Mrs. Singfield were coming and why. You also knew that it would be a test of my faith in you. You saw them coming before they thought about coming. You are a seer of all things. I am trying to stop focusing on the punishing of the Bishop and First Lady along with their flock. There are others like them who have yet to feel your wrath. Although they have used religion to steal from people who come to your house of worship seeking a prophetic word, direction, and your love, you have a way of overseeing all things. Everything is about timing to us, yet you are timeless. I am slowly but surely beginning to understand people like the Bishop and his First Lady, as well as my parents, using your word for monetary gain, material gain, political positioning, Pimpin, and every other self-absorbed act, except spiritual gratification and will one day face your wrath.

Father, please continue helping me to understand your word the way it was meant to be understood without being scathed. Gift me the ability to understand my journey the way you created it for me to understand. I don't doubt that you exist, nor do I doubt your word. What I have an issue with is the way your word was manipulated and changed to validate the opinions and wrong doings by others.

Father, I understand that your word was prophesied and written. What's confusing me is understanding the truth in what was re-written, studied and fought over for thousands of years. I have no understanding of your word being plagiarized, and misinterpreted due to agenda, power, economics, and politics by influential people. Their opinions and different beliefs, not facts, were the basis for their choices and not spirituality. I ask for discernment. Godly discernment to understand all of this through a spiritual eye instead of an eye for an eye.

One last thing Father, I know I get long winded, but I need to ask you for one more thing. Please help me to protect my baby. I am beginning to believe that this is the reason the Bishop and Mrs. Singfield tracked me down. I haven't felt life in my stomach for a couple of days. I need to get situated so that I can find a doctor. Please lead the way and cover me. Amen.

I felt a weight lifted off of me and at peace. I knew that the God within me had me covered and continued working within me. I am a definite work in progress. In the back of my mind, I knew that the devil tried to play advocate. He wanted me to believe that I was continually being punished, he tried planting doubt. Although I do struggle with forgiving the Bishop, First Lady, my parents, and all who have beat, raped, and abused me, I've asked God to guide me and strengthen my heart enough to forgive all those who've violated and abused my body, my trust, and my love.

I lack proper guidance and spiritual obedience. For my age, I have experienced a lot. My teachings about life period were incorrect. I do not trust the teachings and interpretations I grew up accustomed to. I found that they were full of personal opinion, and judgement with little to no facts. This was done in order to justify the choices that were forced upon me. I understood *John 1: 9 reads, "If we confess our sins, he is faithful and just and will forgive us our sins and purify us from all unrighteousness.* But then I also read Mathew 6:15 and it read, *"But if you do not forgive others their sins, your Father will not forgive your sins.*" I don't understand the fairness in this, or why I have to forgive the Bishop, First lady, my parents or the others who raped, abused, and beat me. Maybe with healing and growth in the proper word of God, one day I will understand this. I am all over the place. I want to forgive, if it is the will of God, I just need to learn how. God come through!

I got up and went to my hotel room and began packing. I called an Uber, scheduled a pickup, and asked the Uber driver to notify me when he arrived, he did just that. I went to the front desk, paid my bill, and left. I called Candy back at the management office to explain that I had an emergency issue. She assured me that it was okay and that she was still available. I had the Uber driver take me to her office and leave. I assumed that she was an older lady, but Candy was as young as myself. We laughed and talked before heading out to the property in her company car. As we pulled on the street, I knew right off the back that I would love the home.

Once we arrived, I hadn't had a chance to go inside before I expressed how nice the neighborhood was. The home was beautiful and just the right size for me. Candy explained the credit check process and application process which made me immediately hold my head down. She asked me what was wrong. My head was still down as I began saying, "I have no work history, there is nothing to check. All I have is money. I am new in town, actually I just arrived. I can pay my rent for six months in advance," I stated. I didn't want to tell her that I am too young to have my own place, and that I still have this last year left in high school. We entered the property without Candy saying a word. She walked me around the property and left me in awe.

Candy asked me to give her a moment, she walked off as I continued walking through the home checking out how secure and quaint it was. There were cameras everywhere from the outside into the inside. The back yard was small, yet fenced in. Candy re-entered the room, looked at me sad and said, "I am so sorry! She then burst out with, "THEY SAID YES!!" She tried playing it off but couldn't. She was as excited for me as I was for myself. I signed the contract and gave her the money. I gave her a little extra as she handed me the keys.

I then said, "Thank you Candy for being very professional, and caring. I appreciate you going that extra mile for me."

She looked at me with tear filled eye's and began, "This is a blessing that I was not expecting. I prayed for it, yet I had no idea where my blessing would come from. My son needs medication that I couldn't afford. I have no insurance because I am new on the job. I applied for government insurance but have not been approved yet. I don't know if you believe in God or not, but I prayed for this," she responded. We sat on the floor and talked for a while. I found her to be such an amazing person. Her strength and will to persevere gave me confidence, along with my mustard seed of faith. We vowed that we were going to stick by one another from that day forward. She reminded me of an angel.

Candy helped me further by giving me a list of utility companies that I'd need to call in order to get my utilities on. After she left, I began handling my business. I had an Uber pick me up. My first stop was the post office to get a P.O. Box. I found a Residence Inn close by and paid for a week in advance. While there, I had an opportunity to speak with management and explain that I wanted my stay to be confidential. Next, I went to the license bureau to get a new I.D. After that, I took a break to put some food in my stomach.

The Uber driving stuck around and waited for me because the day was slow. I google searched furniture stores in the area and found one nearby. I found some amazing things, yet I knew that I needed to purchase wisely. I bought my living room and bedroom furnishings, and a small kitchen table and chair set, as well as a couple of televisions. I scheduled the delivery for the next day. I ran by Walmart and bought a list of things from towels, to bedding, more toiletries, dishes, silverware, cups, a George Foreman, Air frier, the works. I also purchased a couple more outfits and personal items because school would be starting soon, and my stomach was getting noticeably bigger.

I am excited about furnishing and decorating. I will do more grocery shopping after the utilities are on. My next goal will be to work on getting my driver's license after school begins. The school may have a Simulator Driving course or discounted rate. If not, I will find a class off of the internet and sign up for driving classes. For now, I just need an I.D., a job, and I am going to try to purchase a car. I will open a savings and save the rest of my money for emergencies and flights back and forth for trial. I almost forgot; I need to contact Attorney Body and ask her to help me find an emancipation attorney.

Chapter Thirteen

The Ending and the Beginning

Before I picked up my phone to call out, Attorney Body was calling me. "Hello, Kenna, this is Attorney Body. How are you?" she asked.

"I am holding on," I responded.

"Good!" she said. "Listen I have a few updates I thought you would be interested in hearing. First, I heard about the incident with the Bishop and Mrs. Singfield showing up in North Carolina. They will be transported back here within a few hours. The detectives were finishing up the paperwork. Charles, or Bishop I should say, obviously was in violation of his bail. Bail will not be an option moving forward. He as well as Mrs. Singfield will also be charged with attempted kidnapping. I wanted to inform you of this because it will be on the news if it hasn't already broadcasted. Both will be on a twenty-three-hour lockdown until trial. Your mother and Deacon Ladson have turned on the others one by one. We have enough evidence on Bishop, The First Lady, and your father to put them away for life. The assistant Bishop and other Deacons have requested a plea deal. I refused the deal. Oh, and before I forget, Mr. Singfield filed for a divorce from his wife. He and Marco are livid and embarrassed. They both wrote statements and brought in evidence of Mrs. Singfields involvement they found tucked away. He has cut out access to his money until the ruling in their divorce is granted. While meeting in my office briefly for business matters, Marco inquired about you. He wanted me to let you know how sorry he was for his mother's actions and wanted to make sure I told you that he loves you," Attorney Body stated.

"Thanks Attorney Body," I began. "Before we hang up, I need your assistance or recommendation on filing my emancipation. I need legal representation in order to file the paperwork. I may also need you to walk me through the process."

"No problem, I will get right on it," Attorney Body responded.

"I should be moved in by the end of the week. I found a beautiful small home," I began. "Oh, and before I forget Attorney Body, how much more are you owed?" I asked.

"Kenna, Mr. Singfield made sure that he paid me enough and then some. You're fine," she stated.

"I am happy about that," I continued. "F.Y.I. Mrs. Singfield made it clear that a few of the flock are backing the Bishop and helped him with bail. She also made mention that members helped them to locate me. Who would do such a thing was my question?" I posed to Attorney Body.

Attorney Body was quiet for a few seconds before she said, "This case has truly pissed me off! Kenna, I am going to fight tooth and nail for you! I will make sure that all parties receive exactly what is coming to them. This case is not only personal for you, but it is personal to me. I don't really discuss my personal business with clients, but in order for you to understand how close to home this hit, I need to expose a little bit to you about myself. Kenna my birth name is Charmain Campbell. My married name is Charmain Campbell-Body. I use my married name, Attorney Body, because I was a product of rape, abuse, molestation, and prostitution. My biological mothers name was Caroline Campbell. She got pregnant by someone in the church at the age of fourteen. After giving birth, she gave the baby away. It just so happens that the baby, who is me, ended up being reared by a great family. I met my biological mother when I turned twenty-one at a church convention. We've seen one another and she knows me, but her presence had no meaning. I felt nothing and nor does she.

"I am so sorry Attorney Body. We can definitely talk more when you have the time or when you are ready," I stated. I felt really bad for Attorney Body. I could hear the pain in her voice. I knew it all so well.

"Maybe we can talk this weekend or sometime during the week," Attorney Body said. I was good with whatever time. Going through what we have both experienced takes a lot of prayer, willpower, and courage.

"Sounds great to me," I began responding. "I will speak with you then," I said as I hung up my line.

I sat and thought about whether or not to call Marco. I really do care about him. I didn't want him to hate me for leaving like I did. I had to make sure that I protected myself along with my baby. Speaking of baby, let me google a nearby Obstetrician. I need to be seen as soon as possible.

After doing a google search and finding an Obstetrician who was less than twenty minutes away, I decided to go ahead and call-in to schedule a new patient appointment. They had an opening for five days from today that I took. The only issue was, I would have to pay cash for everything because I had no insurance. I applied for the states medical insurance online as well as food assistance. It could take seven to ten days' for a response. I needed to try and save money where I could.

I dialed Marco's number and waited nervously as his phone rang. Just as I decided to hang up, I heard his manly baritone voice. "Hello," he said.

"Hello Marco, how are you?"

"May I ask whose speaking?" Marco asked.

That threw me for a loop, so I said, "Uhm, this is Kenna. Has it been that long?"

There was a silence before Marco came back with, "I was just kidding. How are you?"

"I am doing okay," I stated.

"Kenna, I am so sorry for my mother's actions. I should have been honest with you when I found out she was at the church as the secretary. The night I saw her their messed me up. I..."

"Stop Marco! You do not have to explain. I believe you, actually I heard the conversation the night before I left. Honestly, I left because of the conversation that I overheard. I wasn't sure of what was going on,

I just felt that I needed to get away. I needed space, I couldn't think," I said with a sudden sadness.

"I understand Kenna, and probably would have felt the same way. I am not mad at all. I just pray daily for your safety and that I will get to see you again. I love you Kenna," Marco confessed.

I sat on the phone for a couple of seconds before I responded. I wanted to make sure that my response to what he said was honest and true. He was too fragile to be led on or taken advantage of. "I love you more Marco. I always have," I responded back.

Marco and I continued talking and laughing. We caught up on what was going on in one another's lives. Marco continued doing something during our entire conversation that I had to stop and ask him about. He kept putting the phone on mute.

"Why do you keep muting the line Marco?" I asked.

"Well, uhm, my dad, he keeps uhm asking me stuff. You know how parents are," he said through his lying teeth.

He went on to inform me that his father put the house up for sale and was serious about divorcing his mother. His father found out more things about his mother by which he is appalled. He had no previous knowledge of some of the things she was into. She covered up a lot of her life that has been exposed due to this case.

"Have you kept up with the news reports on this case?" Marco asked.

"Not really," I responded.

"My mother and the Bishop will not be allowed to bond out because of the new attempted kidnapping charges. Which was fantastic news for us. The Bishop's followers are more like a cult. They have been marching in front of the justice center, having prayer vigils, and a few showed up over here with torches trying to torch our home, until my dad and I started shooting our guns off. That is part of the reason we are getting out of here," Marco explained.

"That is ridiculous! I am not old enough to get a gun. I wish I were because they'd look like sponges when I was finished," I said. We both laughed.

"Kenna," Marco began. "Will I ever get to see you again?" he asked.

I smiled at the thought of being close to him. I want to see him so badly. "Marco, I would love to see you again soon. I just found a place and won't be able to move in for a day or so," I said.

"Well, it's final," Marco began. "I am coming to help you move and get situated. Send me your information and where you are staying. I will book a flight in the morning to come and help my woman handle her business. We have a couple of weeks left before school starts and I plan to enjoy every moment with you," he stated.

I was so excited that I could hardly think. I began texting him the hotel information, city, and state. "Marco, please do me a favor?" I asked.

"Anything," he said.

"Could you tell your dad that I said thank you so much for everything he has done for me. I genuinely appreciate him," I said.

"Done," Marco responded. "I will text you my flight information once I confirm everything," he began. "Kenna, I love you! You are the strongest woman I have ever known," Marco said before we hung up.

I just laid-back thinking about life, and how it would be if Marco and I were to become an item. What's funny is the fact that he thinks we already are. I caught his remark about "his woman." He is too much. I can't wait to see him; Marco makes me feel safe. The thought of him arriving is exciting! I laid there thinking and praying until I soon drifted off into a deep sleep. I felt hot. Sweat pouring from my body as though I stood next to a fire blazing incinerator. It became hard to breath; I gasped for air barely able to catch my breath. I felt my baby kicking around for the first time in a while. This was the only good sign I received. I struggled to awaken only to awaken to the Bishop standing before me in a blaze of fire. His body burned as he smiled at me. I tried screaming, but nothing would come out. I began praying for God to help me and rebuking Satan. The entire scenario disappeared as the room cooled off. I was able to wake up and look around. Nothing out of the ordinary existed. I must have had a nightmare. I rubbed my stomach and laid still until I drifted back off to sleep.

I was awakened by the morning sun that glared through the window. I thanked God for a new day of awakening and decided to get up, shower, and prepare for my day. My furnishings were going to be delivered, and my electric is scheduled to be turned on today, the gas and water tomorrow. I hadn't heard anything back from Marco, but I did text him my info. I was excited to see him.

I showered and prepared myself for a busy day. I decided to go down to the hotel lobby and grab a bite to eat. While I sat in the lobby, waiting for my Uber and eating a breakfast sandwich, I decided to call Candy. Candy answered the phone sounding muffled. I could barely understand what she was saying before she hung up the line. I didn't know her good enough to say that she sounded strange, but something was definitely off.

The Uber driver sent a text saying that he was out front, so I grabbed my items and headed out to Uber. Candy sent me a text apologizing and saying that she was terribly sorry, and she'd call me as soon as her boyfriend Mike left. I responded back letting her know that I was heading over to the house, and I would love for her to stop by. She didn't text back, so I assumed that he was still there.

Chapter Fourteen

Soul Tie

The electric company arrived about forty-five minutes after I arrived and turned on the electricity. The furnishing truck backed up in the driveway minutes after and began unloading. I held the door open and noticed a Lincoln truck pull up out front. I wasn't sure to whom the truck belonged. Whomever sat there for a few minutes before exiting. I was hoping it was Marco in a rental because it was close to his arrival time, and I still hadn't heard from him. I was unsure as to who it was, until the person exited the car. It was Candy. I was relieved to see her. "Hey girl what's going on!" I yelled out in excitement. She waved to acknowledge my greeting. Candy dressed so cute to me. She was rocking a cute teal Nike cropped jogger, with the matching shoes and cross body. As she approached closer to where I was, I noticed that Candy had a black eye, and a swollen mouth. I looked at her with confusion and concern. She continued walking toward me with a sadness with which I was awfully familiar.

Candy hugged me and cried. I embraced her and allowed her to have her time. I didn't ask her any questions, I just prayed for her as she emotionally released her pain on my shoulders. I wanted her to understand that I wasn't here to judge her, only to support her. When she released me, I held her hand until she released my hand in order to wipe her face. I looked at her and said, "Hey lady, let's go inside." I asked one of the delivery guys to hold the door for the others as Candy and I entered the house. We walked into the kitchen and took a seat on the chairs that belonged to my new kitchen table. The delivery guys laid the table against the wall out of the way.

Candy sat looking so pitiful and lightweight embarrassed. I waited for her to begin the conversation without feeling forced. I wanted her to relax enough to allow her pain to be released as we sat in silence, and I prayed for her.

"Mike has been beating on me Kenna. I think he is cheating, but he will not leave me alone. I've asked him to leave, but he won't. His abusive ass tried forcing me to have sex with him and I refused him. I wasn't trying to do crap with the cheater! He began punching me in my stomach and smacking me around. I got tired of it and found a way to run into the kitchen without him being able to stop me. I started throwing glasses and dishes at him. I hit Mike in the back of his head with a mason jar and watched the blood drip down over his clothing. This truly pissed him off to the point of him calling me every name under the sun. I didn't care about none of that, but something did tell me to stay in the kitchen, and I did just that. I had a small pot on the stove that I fried French fries in earlier. I turned the grease on and let it get hot. I kept my eyes on him as he walked around looking for the keys to my other car. My keys and my phone were both under a pillow on the couch. Mike began throwing the pillows at me and saying how much he hated me. That's when he noticed my keys and phone. Surprisingly, he did not bother the phone, but he took my car keys. Just as he opened my door, I ran over and pushed him out and threw hot grease on his ass. I was able to lock the door behind him. He screamed and began running in circles outside the door. I watched as he tried removing his shirt that was stuck to his skin. He was going into shock, at least that's how it appeared. I watched him further jump in my car and pull off driving erratically. I called the police and filed a police report. I also reported my car stolen and the assault. I wanted to come by and let you know what was going on before I head to Walmart to buy new locks," Candy stated.

"I am so sorry this has happened to you. You do not have to return; you can stay here for a few days or at the hotel. Candy, abuse is a terrible thing to endure. I have been abused all of my life. I never told you my story, but that is the reason I am here."

Candy looked at me in shock before saying, "WHAT!" I shook my head to confirm what she was thinking. "I am so sorry for you Kenna," Candy began. I am happy that I met you though, you are the friend I never had. I wanted to stop by so that you wouldn't worry. I have errands to run, so I can't stay," Candy stated.

I stared at her with love and sympathy filled eyes. She looked horrible, and I feared for her safety. "If you will not take me up on my offer to crash out here or at the hotel, promise me that you will call me and check in," I requested.

"Pinky promise," she responded as she left out.

I decided to go and put the toiletries I bought away and make up my bed. I walked around the back end of the house to my bedroom, humming away. I was startled by a shadow standing off the door. I proceeded over to where I saw the reflection, and there was nothing and no one there. Maybe it is my nerves. I need to get something to eat and drink and possibly lay down for a second.

I entered the kitchen and noticed that the delivery guys had wrapped up and were just about ready to pull off. My paperwork was laid on the floor at the entrance of the house, so I picked it up and set it on the table. I began making a couple of peanut butter and jelly sandwiches, and was just about done, when I felt pain in the bottom of my stomach and nausea. I became nervous because I was unsure of what to do. The pain was so severe that I left my food on the table, rushed over to the couch, and laid down. I felt pressure followed up by sharp pains between my legs. God help me! Before I could feel anything else, I regurgitated. It brought some relief, but not a lot. I was still leery of getting up and my face and body were drenched in sweat. All I was able to do was hang slouched off of the couch.

"Kenna are you okay?" Marco shouted as he entered my unlocked screen door. I was so excited to see Marco. He immediately dropped his bags at the entrance and came over to where I laid. I began crying as I tried to explain to him how nauseous I felt, along with the pain.

Marco immediately got back up and suggested that I lay in my room. He carried me to the back and laid me in my bed as he went into my bathroom and retrieved a cool wet rag, which he applied to my face. He went into the kitchen and brought my food along with a nice cold ginger ale. Marco took my small trash can out of the bathroom and set it next to my bed with a bag in it. This was just in case my stomach began hurting again. He then climbed on the bed next to me and held me close. He rubbed on my stomach a little as though the baby I was carrying was his and not the Bishops. I ended up dozing off to sleep and awoke to a foul odor. I lifted my head and looked around the room. I swear I saw a shadow of something, or someone walk away. The smell dissipated like it never existed. Marco was sound asleep. My bladder felt full, so I jumped up to go to the restroom, and that is when I saw it. I was bleeding. I stopped and yelled for Marco to awaken. He jumped up startled and confused, not knowing what was going on or where he was for a split second. Once he got his bearings together he was able to understand me asking him to take me to a hospital.

Marco helped me get dressed and walked me to his rental car in a matter of minutes. He was more nervous than I. Although it was a little late, I thought about Candy and that I hadn't spoken back to her since she left. I figured it wouldn't hurt to text her to make sure that she was safe. I also wanted to let her know that we were heading over to the hospital. As I glanced down at the phone, I noticed that she had called my phone five times and text me to call her A.S.A.P. ten times.

"Oh my God," I said out loud. I never heard either while I was asleep. I tried not to panic or overreact.

"What's wrong Babe?" Marco asked.

"Do you remember the girl I spoke to you about who helped me get my place?" I asked him.

"Yes, Candy," he responded back.

"Yes," I began. "Her boyfriend has been abusing her. Earlier she quickly visited, and I noticed her eyes and face were swollen. Her boyfriend not only physically abused her, but mentally she suffered as well. Somehow she found out that he was cheating on her, she asked him to leave, and things spun out of control. He ended up beating up on her. Somehow she was able to get away from him and ran into the kitchen. From what she said, he decided that he was going to take her other vehicle without her permission and leave, so he searched for her keys. While he searched and continued verbally attacking her, she was able to turn the stove on and warm up some grease she already had sitting on top of the stove. Just as he found her keys under a pillow on her couch, and opened the door to leave, she drenched him with the hot grease and was able to push him out of the door and lock it," I explained.

Marco didn't say too much of anything except, "I pray she is okay."

We pulled up into the Emergency area of the hospital and noticed how busy it was. I was not up for sitting here all night, but I knew I needed to get checked out because something just wasn't right. We entered and registered in the Emergency room area where we were instructed to have a seat. We were told that someone would come out and get me when it was my turn.

Marco and I made petty talk as we watched the Emergency room fill up. "It must be a full moon out tonight," Marco stated.

I said, "Right!" as I began texting Candy's phone and awaiting a reply. "I hope she is okay," I blurted out. "I offered her my hotel room seeing that I paid for the entire week. I still have a couple of days there that are already paid for. Speaking of that, I need to get the rest of my items from there. The Gas and water get switched over at the house in the morning. Although the water and gas are on, the companies have to come out and do reads on the meters in order to begin my service and end the owners service," I said.

As I continued rattling on about the lists of things I still needed to handle, Marco listened on. Something stopped my train of thought and caught my eye. I watched as the paramedics rushed through pushing someone covered in blood under a white sheet. It was the shoes I saw. The teal Nike's. "Please God, no! Please just let it be a coincidence," I mumbled. Marco looked from me to where he saw me looking. Tears started to drop from my eyes. Just as I jumped up to try and see if that was Candy, the paramedics slid through the door. A nurse appeared at the same door and called my name. Marco made me sit back down in the wheelchair that was given us at registration. He pushed me through the door, and the nurse took over pushing from that point.

The nurse tried making small talk, yet I wasn't in the small talk mood. I looked around as I was pushed to see where they had taken the body. The nurse took me into a room, asked me one hundred questions, gave me a gown, and said the doctor would be in to see me. Marco and I both dozed off as we waited.

Chapter Fifteen

Death Is So Final

I awoke to hearing alarms going off and "Code Blue" being announced over an intercom. Nurses and doctors were scattering back and forth. I grabbed my IV pole and walked to the entrance in order to see where everyone was running to. I couldn't decipher what was going on, so I decided to walk in the direction of the guy's wearing black jackets with "Johnson's Funeral Home" printed on the back. They were headed in the opposite direction as of everyone else. I stood and watched as they walked into a room that was two rooms down from where I was. I continued watching as they transferred what appeared to be a dead body onto another flat bed. The men in the funeral jackets spoke to someone who appeared to be a nurse, signed a few papers, and began wheeling the bed with the person out of the room.

I saw those shoes again and decided to walk up to the guys. "May I help you?" One of the guys asked as he saw me approaching closer. I stood for a second unsure of whether I was prepared to handle this if it were Candy or not. "Miss, can we help you? If not, could you please move over so that we can transport this body please?" the gentleman asked.

"I'm, I'm sorry sir, but I, uhm think this is my friend. Can I, uhm...," I was stuck. I couldn't ask nor could I walk away. I reached over and lifted the sheet and recognized Candy. Candy had been beaten severely. I wanted to scream but couldn't. Tears ran down my face as I walked backward back to my room. Once I made it back to my bed I cried uncontrollably. The pain I felt at this moment superseded the pain I was having that brought me here. "I'm going to kill him! I'm going to freakin kill him myself! I cried and cried until I couldn't cry any longer. I had no idea that Marco had awakened and was trying to comfort me nor that the doctor was standing beside me. I had lost it!!

"Baby, what's wrong? Who are you wanting to kill?" Marco asked. The doctor appeared as confused as Marco.

"Marco," I began. "Candy is dead! That was her the paramedics brought in through emergency. She tried calling me and texting me, remember I told you? I tried texting her back, and she never replied back. Oh my God, I feel horrible about this. She needed my help, and I wasn't there to help her. I don't even think she has family to care for her sick son, oh my God Marco!" I cried out, yet I had no more tears left in me. Marco just hugged me tight without saying a word.

The doctor took that opportunity to step around us and asked, "Miss Ricks, is it okay that I take your vitals, and possibly do an ultrasound?" I wanted to say no but thought against it. I shook my head "yes" and sat back on the bed in order to get this over with. I wanted to get back to the house or hotel whichever Marco could get us to first.

The doctor took my vitals which were a little high, not high enough to cause concern. As he completed that task, a nurse wheeled in an ultrasound machine and prepared me for an ultrasound. "Well," she said as she watched the monitor, somebody is headfirst and working themselves down into the canal. What you may have experienced were contractions dear," she stated.

"Contractions!?" I thought out loud. "But how, why? I have a few more months to go," I said to no one in particular.

The nurse smiled before saying, "Well honey, we have no control over the Lords will. This baby is coming when she wants to," she stated. Her weight is six pounds and fourteen ounces, so her weight poses no danger. I will speak with the doctor Miss Ricks, to see if he wants to check and see if you've dilated.

"Marco, I am not ready! I haven't had the opportunity to shop for the baby. There is so much happening around me right now, I feel like I am losing it."

Marco stood next to my bed and said," Kenna, I need you to relax. You are over thinking everything. I am here right now to help alleviate some of your stress and tension if you'll let me. We also need to pray, Praying seems to calm the mood," he said. I smiled at him before starting my prayer.

"Father, I come to you with a humbled yet troubled heart. I understand that your word say's, you are close to the brokenhearted, and you save those who are crushed. You promise that you are closer than we realize and can heal our hearts. I need healing pronto! Like yesterday Father!

I'm so tired of crying and struggling with no clarity. I need you to speak through me father. I need my life radically changed. Have your way with me father. I need your strength and your power to stand in me. I want to overcome the discomfort I've endured and suffered immensely. I've done this in order to manifest my purpose. I am looking for my purpose, yet I don't understand why you created me.

I am uncomfortable, sad, depressed with feelings of inadequacy. I am beginning to realize that suffering comes with growth. Father, I want to grow, I want to understand my purpose and feel enthusiastic about it. Yet I know that suffering is a part of reality. I am so tired of suffering father. Please step in and help me. In your name father, I ask that you cover me, lead, protect and guide me. Amen!"

"Amen," Marco repeated. The doctor entered the room shortly after to do an examination to see if I dilated and lost my mucus plug. Everything was intact. I was given orders to follow up with an Obstetrician and to take it easy. The doctor said that I was having Braxton Hicks contractions. He gave me a prescription for prenatal vitamins and explained how important my diet and taking them were. I thanked him and began dressing before he could get out of my room good.

Marco and I drove to the hotel and decided we would stay there at least for the night. We both wanted a nice hot shower and a good night's rest. Marco went in the restroom first to shower, so I busied myself laying out my pajamas and a few other items. He had nothing there because his bag was at the house. He decided to slip back on his underwear after he showered. As he dried off, my bladder couldn't hold out.

"Marco, I need to come in and use it," I said. Marco opened the door, and I sat on the toilet relieving myself. I tried not to look in his direction, but I peeked and almost fainted. Marco was built. He stood about six foot three or four, Marco was bronze with curly hair. He had a perfect smile and a body of a God. He tried to cover himself up, so I turned away. He walked out of the restroom before me. I flushed, washed my hands, and returned to get my pajamas and other items.

I quickly showered and brushed my teeth. I jumped in the bed to snuggle up under Marco. Marco pulled me in close to him and began rubbing my stomach as well as kissing my neck. I turned to face him. I wanted to look at him and appreciate him in the moment. I kissed his lips, and he kissed me back. We began kissing and touching one another hungrily. We were interrupted by my phone ringing. I grabbed my phone while Marco still had me wrapped in his arms. It felt awkward, but good at the same time.

"Hello," I said.

"Hello Kenna. How are you? Is this an inconvenient time?" Attorney Body asked.

I thought to myself, "Uhh yeah it is missy," but I knew not to say that.

"Well," she began. "I have some good news and some all-right news. Your mother and Deacon Ladson submitted enough solid evidence against the Bishop, First Lady, and your father to put them away for life. In exchange, those two were given ten solid years with no opportunity for parole. Mrs. Singfield did not want to go to trial. We meet tomorrow morning. She is looking at seven years with no opportunity for parole. The Assistant Bishop is giving us a challenging time. His

Attorney wants him out on bail. He is trying to say that you came on to him," Attorney body stated.

"Wow," was all that I could think to say. Attorney Body went on to say although she tried blocking him from bailing out, it is ultimately up to the judge. The trial dates have been set for the Bishop, First Lady, and the Assistant Deacon for two months from now.

The only thing I could think to say was, "Okay."

"Kenna, before I forget, I filed your emancipation papers for you. I asked a friend of mines to push them through. I explained that you have relocated and may not be able to travel to court due to you being pregnant. Hopefully, you should have your papers here soon," she stated.

"Thank you so much Attorney Body. I genuinely appreciate your help. No problem Kenna. Take care of yourself," she said.

"I will," I responded.

I turned back to face Marco, and he was snoring lightly. I didn't want to bother him; I knew he was tired. I snuggled back under him and decided to lay here until I drifted off to sleep.

The morning came quickly. When I awoke, I got up and opened up the sliding glass doors. I wanted to smell the morning air and listen to the birds chirp. I stood and looked out thanking God for a new day. As I stood on the patio, I had an eerie feeling. I looked around at nothing in particular. For a second, I thought I saw Marco, but he is in the room sleeping. I swear my eyes were playing tricks on me. Whomever it was, vanished as fast as they appeared. I found that very odd. I closed the door back along with the curtains. By then Marco was up just watching me and smiling. I told him what I had just observed. Marco got up and went to look for himself. Whomever it was were gone. He wore a look of frustration, but never said a word.

Marco and I decided to get dressed and head down to the breakfast buffet to get some food and a little coffee. We were well aware of the time because we had a lot to accomplish today. Thank God Marco had a rental car, it saved me money. After we ate, we headed over to the house to meet the gas and water company. They came right on time. After they left, Marco drove me over to the License Bureau to get an I.D. as well as over to the school to register. The school I will be attending is called West High.

Lunch time was approaching, and I began getting hungry. Marco and I ran and picked up my prescriptions next. I announced to Marco that I was ready to get a bite to eat. He is such a sweet guy, I thought. It is easy to fall in love with him. We headed over to Wasabi's Restaurant across the street. I had a taste for some shrimp, steak, and chicken stir fry. After we laughed and ate, we headed to the grocery store to fill up on groceries. We also went and checked out of the hotel. I turned my key in while Marco went to the car to wait. When I came out, he was nowhere in sight. I stood outside of the car and waited for approximately fifteen minutes or so. I noticed he was coming around from the side of the hotel limping a little.

"Sorry about that babe," he said as he unlocked the doors.

"It's okay. Where did you go?" Marco's hands were shaking, and I noticed bruising. I never said a word about it.

"When I came out to the car to put the last load in, a couple of characters approached me at the car and tried to run a scam. One of the guys actually swung on me and I blasted him in his nose. I chased them behind the hotel," he said.

"Oh my God are you okay?" I asked. "Marco, you could have gotten hurt honey, you have to be careful," I stated.

"I will babe," is all he said. We headed over to our last stop which was Walmart. We bought some groceries, a baby bed, changing table, car seat, sleepers, outfits, rags, wipes, diapers, you name it. We were so loaded down that we could hardly see to drive.

I was dead tired after all of that. We decided to call it a day and head back to the house. I noticed that Marco was going in the wrong direction, so I said, "Marco, I thought that we were finished for the day. I am dead tired and ready to go home," I continued.

"We are going to the house Babe, what are you talking about?" he asked.

"Well, if that's the case, you are going in the wrong direction," I responded. Marco pulled over in the gas station while I put my GPS on. The GPS got us home in no time.

I helped Marco as best I could to bring in the groceries and put them away. While I still felt up to it, I also put away the items I bought and had at the hotel. After I finished, I helped Marco in the babies room. Marco set the baby's bed up after he assembled it and the changing table. "You did surprisingly good putting these together Marco, I thought you said that you were horrible with stuff like this," I said more as a statement than a question. He just snickered and kept on working away, his hands and arms shook quite a bit. Marco may need to get himself checked out, I thought. I put some of the diapers and wipes under the changing table and the rest in the closet along with the outfits. We made up the baby's bed, took all the boxes out, and headed to the room. I was dead tired. I laid back on the bed and just relaxed.

"Would you like me to fix you some juice or lemonade?" Marco asked.

"Please," I responded. I laid in the bed until Marco walked back in and handed me my lemonade and my prenatal vitamin. I wanted to sleep cuddled up under him and have a relaxing night.

Chapter Sixteen

Everything Is Not What It Appears

M

arco laid next to me and turned on the game. As I drifted off to sleep, I felt him cuddle with me. I awoke sometime later with the worst cramps I have ever had, and I was bleeding again. This was the worst pain that I have ever experienced in my life. I felt pressure between my legs like the baby was exiting on its own. I began sweating profusely and regurgitating until I couldn't do anything but dry heave. Marco jumped up and got me a wet towel and also cleaned up the mess.

"We need to get you back to the hospital," he stated. I got up and washed up as best I could, before heading back to the hospital. This time was different. The pain was coming every couple of minutes. These must be contractions, I thought. We arrived at the hospital in record time. They took me back immediately with no hesitation. A nurse took me into a birthing room and hooked me up to a machine that displayed my contractions and heart rate. They took my vitals and did everything needed to prepare me for delivery of my baby. I was nervous because it was too early for her to come. The doctor came in and began assuring me that I would be okay. I was still frightened. I wanted my mommy. I wanted to cry so bad because it hurt. The doctor came in and looked at the monitor as he took a seat in front of me. He introduced himself and explained the process. The nurse asked me if I wanted an epidural and I said no. I was scared and had no idea what it was, even after they explained. The doctor and nurses put my legs in the stirrups and the doctor began checking between my legs to see how far I had dilated and checking to see if the baby's head had crowned. I began feeling the contractions again and started crying again. "These hurts so bad," I said.

"You will be okay. The baby's head is crowning, you are ten centimeters on the nose. When you get your next contraction, I want you to push okay," the doctor said. Just as he said it, a strong contraction came, and I pushed as hard as I could. The doctor said, "Great job. When you feel the next one give me a real big push okay," he said once again. Marco stood off to the side watching, he never said a word. He just watched and shook.

"One is coming," I said.

"Push, push, one more time, push hard," he said. I felt a plop and a baby cry. It was over.

They cleaned her up and laid her on my chest. I began thanking God for this beautiful creation. Although the circumstances behind her birth were horrific, she is such a beautiful and adorable blessing. Tears fell as I promised her that I would love and protect her. The doctors congratulated me and asked me had I chosen a name for her. I looked at her and didn't see a trace of the Bishop. She looked like my twin. Her hair was thick and long, her face was perfect. She was perfect. I could see my mother's ancestry in her features. I decided to name her Angel. "Angel, her name is going to be Angel Yahushua Ricks," I said.

"Beautiful name," the nurses and doctor said.

Marco came over and rubbed her head and along her body. He was gentle with her. "Would you like to hold her?" I asked him. Marco had a terrified look on his face. Although I was glad that he was here, I began to worry about him. I noticed that he hadn't taken his medication not one time.

He responded, "No thanks, I will just look. Babies frighten me," he said with a half of a smile.

After leaving my Angel with us in the room for several hours, the nurse returned to take her to the nursery. I decided that while she was out of the room, I had a little free time for a nap and to call the management office and find out if arrangements were made for Candy. I also wanted to know who had her son. I dialed them up and a really sweet lady answered the phone. I told her who I was and that I was inquiring about Candy. She was very hesitant to say anything at first. I explained that her and I were good friends and that I was in the hospital with complications and unable to contact her when this happened.

She whispered, "Candy has no family or friends on record. From what I know, Candy was being cremated and her son was in Child Protective Services," she said.

"Oh my God," thank you so much I stated.

The nice lady went on to say, "You know they never found that boyfriend of hers."

"Again, thank you," I said before hanging up the line. I was upset all over again. I laid on my side and cried myself to sleep.

"Cast all of your cares and worries upon me my child. I am the comforter. Worry is a sign of doubt in the goodness that I represent in your life. I am your refuge and strength, and I am ever-present in troubled times.

"Not realizing it, I began thanking God in my sleep. I went from that to trying to figure out if I should go and rescue Candy's son from the Children's home, which is where Child Protective Services most likely took him. How could I maintain with two kids, court, school, and life?

I awoke to Marco leaving out of the room. "Where are you headed Marco?" I asked. He had a look of shock and nervousness upon his face, I wonder what is going on with him.

"Oh uhm, I'm going down to the cafeteria to get me a drink and uhm, I may step outside and get some fresh air," he stated. I shook my head to say okay, but it is definitely something going on with him. I have no time for foolishness, nor will I make time. I have Angel and myself to worry about. He can take himself back home early for all I care.

Marco was gone for several hours, which didn't sit well with me at all. He came back in the room like he hadn't did a thing wrong. He brought me and himself a sprite and put mines on my table. When I went to grab it, I noticed that the cap was broken from the bottle.

Now, I am suspicious. I sat it back down and pretended as though I was watching television. After a few minutes, I noticed he kept watching me.

"Aren't you going to drink your soda?" he asked. I continued watching television like I hadn't heard a word he said. He waited a minute or two and asked me again.

"I am not thirsty!" I said. I continued watching the television and him out of the corner of my eye. I noticed that he was fidgeting with his fingers a lot. My only thoughts at that time was, Marco doesn't want these problems. He may want to go back home and chill for a while before he tries pulling anything over me.

Time had passed with neither of us saying too much of anything. It was getting late, and I was getting tired. The nurse came in and asked me did I want Angel in my room for the night, or did I want her to stay in the nursery. I chose the nursery. I figured she'd be safe in there if anything jumped off.

"Would you like to come visit with her before it gets any later," she asked.

"I sure would," I stated. I got up out of the bed, put another gown around the back of me that was on my chair, and allowed the nurse to push me down to the nursery in a wheelchair. When I looked behind me, I noticed that Marco was tagging along.

We entered the nursery, and I noticed a strange look on the nurses face, yet she continued to walk toward where Angel was being held. There was another nurse holding her and rocking her back and forth.

"Hello," the nurse said to the other. Miss Ricks is here to spend a little time with her baby." The nurse holding Angel looked up like she had an instant attitude. She immediately changed her disposition after seeing the look I had on my face. Marco just stood in place with no emotion one way or the other. The nurse handed me my baby and walked off. She never said hi, sorry, my mistake, or gave an apology for being rude.

I looked at my baby's face, and she truly reminded me of an angel. She was perfect in every way. I sang her a lullaby as I laid her on my chest and rocked her back and forth to sleep. I also watched Marco fidgeting around like he had Parkinson's. He wouldn't stop shaking. I followed his eyes to the nurse who had wheeled me down here having a discussion with someone else, possibly the head nurse. She returned minutes later letting us know that the nursery was about to close up for visiting. I could still take my baby with me if I chose to. Against my better judgement, I thought that she would be safer in the nursery. I kissed Angel and tucked her in. The nurse wheeled me back to the room, and I decided that I would just turn over and get some rest. There was no need in arguing with or continuing to watch Marco looking weird. I was a little excited because I could go home in the morning after the doctor comes to sign off on the paperwork.

I turned over in bed facing away from Marco and heard my cellphone ring. "Hello," I answered.

"Hello Kenna, how are you?" Attorney Body inquired.

"I am okay Attorney Body. I just gave birth to a healthy baby girl," I stated. There was a slight pause before she went on.

"Congratulations," she said. I smiled like a chia pet.

"Thank you," I said.

"I am not going to hold you up. I just wanted to let you know that your emancipation papers were expedited and approved. I can e-mail you copies that you can print at a library and send your originals in the mail if that will be okay with you?" I was so happy!

"Yes, that sounds fine," I said.

"Good, I will get right on it. Other than the baby being born, are you okay?" she asked. I didn't want to say too much. I knew Marco was listening.

"Yes, I am fine. Although, I have been all over the place. I lost the only friend that I made down here to domestic violence. Her boyfriend beat her to death. I feel horrible because she tried calling me that day.

It was a day that I was sick. I fell asleep early and did not hear the calls or texts. The sad part about all of it is, she has a son who is ill. He was in Child Protective Services, and I am fairly sure they've taken him to the Children's Home," I began saying. "I want to fight for him, but I am unsure of how the courts would respond to my request because of my age," I said.

"Being a parent is a lot of responsibility, especially at your age and having a newborn, let alone two kids," Attorney Body said. I became quiet. That is not what I wanted to hear; I began thinking. In my head, once I get out of here, I planned to try and establish a relationship with him, and a report with the staff. If it's meant to be, God will make a way for me.

"Kenna, are you there?" Attorney Body asked.

"Yes," I answered.

"A few more things before I get off the phone. The Assistant Bishop was released on bail with stipulations that he is not to come in contact with you or contact you in any form. He is also not allowed to leave the state. There was something else, let me see here, oh, how could I forget to ask you? Did Marco finally make it to see you okay?" Attorney Body asked. Before I could answer her question, she continued saying, "He was pissed that he missed the first flight and had to catch the next flight out? I had never heard him so angry before. He was fussing about having to purchase a new ticket because his original ticket, along with his phone, and ID went missing. He said that he couldn't call you because he did not know your number by memory. He called me on his burner phone. He mentioned that he retrieved my number from his father. I did give him your address and burner number. I wanted you to know just in case a number pops up that you do not recognize," she said all in one breath. "Have fun and enjoy him. If he contacts me I will tell him that you are at the hospital and have delivered the baby," she continued.

"WHAT!? So, who is th-" Lights out! I felt a blow to my head that knocked me unconscious. Marco would never hurt me. He loved me too much, at least that's what I thought. Attorney Body said that Marco took a later flight, so is this Marco or someone else who apparently looks and sounds exactly like him?

Chapter Seventeen

Darkness Brought To The Light

E verything went dark, I could hear movement and then alarms going off. But I couldn't wake up. Why am I back here? Did I die? I felt that I was in a familiar place, so I assume I've been here before. It was a spiritual realm that had no beginning and no end. It was so beautiful and peaceful in the midst of nowhere. God, if it's not in your will to send me back into my physical shell, could you please cover Angel?

I am so ready to surrender! If it weren't for Angel, I wouldn't want to go back, I am tired of fighting. I feel like I am battling the world alone. I am mentally and emotionally drained. God, I know you know best, and you give your toughest battles to your strongest soldiers, but God, I am tired! I can't take anymore. I am tired of walking through the fire, I am sick of being abused and suffering. God, enough is enough, please step in and help me. I want to elevate my belief in order to walk in my Godly discernment, but Father I have nothing left. I want to ask for forgiveness for my thoughts and give thanks to you anyway. Giving glory to you for my life and allowing me to have Angel. I am trying so hard. Father, if I may be honest, I hated most of that life. I know that the word "hate" is a strong word, but it's true. I want to go back with a knew mindset and outlook if it's in your will. I want to experience your love the way a true believer who stands on your word experiences it. I need to hear directly from you. I thank you for your mercy and grace. In the past, as far back as I can remember, I wanted to die! Father, you allowed me to walk in darkness, experiencing being dead on the inside, losing friends, having no real family, living a life of torture and pain, and yet, I am still here. I want to be born again.

God are you listening? I can't wake up! God, please let me wake up just one more time. Please father! Father, I know you've given me plenty of opportunities to get things right, and I tried! I have to go back this time, my baby has no one else. Oh my God, I am begging you! I laid in place empty, dead with no soul.

I could hear, "Stat, stat." And people running around.

"She has a light pulse. We are losing her. Kenna can you hear me?" someone asked. In my mind, I shook my head, yes. Alarms began going off as I heard across the loudspeaker AMBER ALERT! AMBER ALERT! Another person announced, "CODE BLUE! CODE BLUE!" on the speaker, it wasn't registering. My head was hurting so bad, I couldn't think. It felt swollen, but numb. The doctor was working on me with urgency.

Attorney Body

"Hello, this is Attorney Body, my client's name is Kenna Ricks. I was just speaking with her on the phone, and then there was nothing. I tried calling back and no one answered. It sounded as though there was commotion in the background before the phone dropped. I want to make sure that everything is okay."

"Hello, Attorney Body, let me connect you to the nurses station with the attending physician."

"Okay, thank you."

"This is Dr. Talley; how can I help you?"

"Hello, Dr. Talley. My name is Attorney Body and Kenna Ricks is my client. I am calling back because I was on the phone with her, and something went wrong. I'm not sure if it was a phone issue, or if she suddenly became ill or what. I tried calling back and there was no answer."

"Hello, Attorney Body. Sorry that I am unable to give you any information at this time. I would be in violation of the HIPPA Law. I'm sure you understand. Please contact Detective Evans at 330-777-9311. He can better assist you."

"Wait a damn minute! I do understand. Do you know what, never mind! Enjoy your night!"

"Hello, this is Attorney Body. May I speak with Detective Evans please?"

"This is Detective Evans. How can I help you?"

"My client's name is Kenna Ricks, Detective Evans. She just delivered a baby at Citizens Hospital. I was speaking with her on the phone when all of a sudden there was nothing. I tried calling back and no one answered. It sounded as though there was commotion in the background before the phone dropped. I wanted to make sure that everything was okay. I dialed the hospital's information line back and identified myself, but hey transferred the call to the attending physician, Dr. Talley. He explained that he was unable to give me any information and directed me to you. Can you please tell me what the hell is going on?"

"Hello Attorney Body. I am sorry for all of that, but as an Attorney you are aware that we have to follow procedure. Miss Ricks is fighting for her life as we speak. A nurse went into her room after noticing her vitals setting the systems alarm off at the nurses station. When she walked in Miss Ricks room, she discovered that Miss Ricks had been attacked," the detective began. I immediately went into panic mode. As calm and collected as I always am, this time it was different.

"Detective, I am on my way! Can we meet once I am there? I want to check in on the baby first. I will apply for Power of Attorney over both. Kenna has no one else," I lied and stated.

The detective paused for a moment before saying, "The baby has disappeared. Someone has taken her."

I almost lost my cool! How did that happen, or why were my next thoughts? "I will contact you back after I book my flight," I said as I immediately hung up my line.

I booked my flight and called the detective back with my information. I ran home, grabbed everything I thought I would need and then some. I packed my back and headed straight to the airport. I tried relaxing and praying. For some reason, I knew that Kenna would be okay. I was worried about the baby.

My plane landed. I decided to rent a car versus calling an Uber. I figured it would save me time and money. I put the address to the Police Department in my GPS and headed straight there. Detective Evans awaited my arrival and greeted me at the entrance. We had small talk until we arrived at his office where we got straight down to business.

I explained the entire situation to Detective Evan's regarding Kenna and her case. I also familiarized him on the attempted kidnapping that happened upon her arrival, in which he had a record of on his desk. He informed me, "There was a gentleman who brought

Miss Ricks into the hospital and stayed with her the entire time. He wasn't very talkative, but he was there to support her. A nurse who worked the nursery where baby Angel was accosted for over fifteen years, stated that he acted a little strange to her. She thinks Miss Ricks noticed his demeanor as well, based off of the looks she gave him and another nurse who had no valid credentials to even be back in the area. What is not making sense to me, is the fact that the cameras caught the young man leaving the room hurriedly, and there is no trace of him anywhere. He was seen on camera leaving out of her room a few times, only once for an extended period of time. For the most part, he was her only real visitor. The nurse was seen on camera leaving, but she disappeared off of camera as well. I think both the young man and the fake nurse are working together. I think he hit Miss Ricks in the head for whatever reason, and the nurse took the baby. My question is why? Why was she targeted and set up? Who's behind this fiasco?" he questioned. We both just sat there looking clueless.

"Detective Evan's, I need to see the film of the guy leaving. It could have been Marco. He was coming to visit her. Marco supposedly missed his flight. He called me because he had to book another flight out and was having a challenging time. I also need to see Kenna. Is either or both possible?" I asked.

"Yes, I have the film here, and I will take you over to the hospital myself. Give me a minute," Detective Evans responded.

"That's fine. In the meantime, I need to make an important phone call," I stated.

"Hello Mr. Singfield," I began.

"Hello Attorney Body. How can I help you?" he asked. "Mr. Singfield, you and I have caught up on everything but one situation from the past that I think is coming back to hunt everyone," I began. "Marco maybe in trouble because of it. Remember when we sat and talked in my office, and you practically begged me to be honest with you about a part of my life that I rarely speak of? You showed me my birth certificate with tear filled eye's and I had to explain to you that the monster you married Caroline Campbell Singfield was my biological mother, and Bishop Charles Jackson was my biological father? She gave me to a family in the church when she had me because she was only fourteen years old and pregnant by Charles. Caroline was a product herself of molestation, abuse, rape, and prostitution. Until this day, she refuses to acknowledge she gave birth to me. You then exposed the fact that you weren't Marco's biological father. The reality was that you couldn't have kids. Caroline was cheating on you and ended up pregnant by the First Ladies brother, Assistant Bishop Larry Brown, who happens to be Marco's biological father.

"I remember the conversation," Mr. Singfield stated.

"Mr. Singfield, you made mention that Caroline had three kids. Where is the third one?" I asked. It was complete silence. You could hear a pin drop that's how quiet it had gotten. "Mr. Singfield, I am going to ask you one last time, and I promise I won't ask again. What happened to the third child?" I spoke.

"He escaped the asylum," Mr. Singfield began. "When they were babies, it was a lot for me to care for another man's children. Especially a set of identical twins. Caroline was never here to help, and I was losing it. My sister was great with kids and asked me to send him to her. Marco and Mark are identical twins. Both suffered mental illness, Mark's was much worse and more extreme. He has Schizophrenia, Obsessive Compulsive Disorder, and Borderline Personality Disorder. Marco was just Bipolar and suffered depression at times. As Mark grew up, he became too much of a responsibility for my sister to handle. She was able to afford to put him in a Mental Asylum that genuinely cared for him. When my sister passed away, she left a lot of money for his caretakers. Caroline decided then and only then that she wanted to be a piece of a mother and a caretaker. She took it upon herself behind my back to visit him and tell him who she really was. He had no previous memory of her or knowledge. She showed him baby pictures of him alone with her that were really her and Marco. She had him moved from one place to another and would buy him in order for him to like her. One day, she thought it was a bright idea to bring him here to meet his identical twin he also had no knowledge of. That didn't go over as planned. Neither liked the other, but Mark remembered where we stayed and would come here when he would see Marco leave. When Caroline got arrested, she called and told Mark that Marco's girlfriend got her in a little trouble and mommy dearest wouldn't be able to get him for a while. He was pissed off and began causing serious issues for the other patients at the Asylum. They were scared of him, he wanted out! Last I knew, they were trying to keep him sedated and calm. I haven't had any recent updates," Mr. Singfield explained. I was completely floored.

"May I ask you one more question Mr. Singfield?"

"Yes," he stated, sounding shaken up by now.

"How can you tell them apart," I asked. Mr. Singfield didn't immediately answer.

Finally, he said, "I can't."

"I asked you this because either Marco or Mark has almost killed Kenna. She is in the hospital again fighting yet one more time for her life. She was struck over the head after she had the baby. She had a baby girl named Angel. Marco or Mark has been up here with her the entire time, they are missing, and the baby is also missing.

Chapter Eighteen

Making a Way Out of No Way

I hung up with a visibly shaken Mr. Singfield. He has been caught up in a web of lies because of his wife. It was just in time; Detective Evans re-entered his office. He pulled out his hand-held video camera so that I could view the film of Marco or Mark leaving in and out, as well as the supposed nurse in the babies room.

"Can I get a close up of her please?" I asked. I've seen her face before.

I explained the entire conversation I had to Detective Evans that I had with Mr. Singfield. We both walked in silence and in deep thought as we headed out of his office and to the car. It hit me! I began thinking about whether or not I will be allowed to still represent Kenna in court against my own biological mother, or will she let the cat out of the bag, and it becomes a conflict of interest? I may have to recuse myself from this case. I can't take any chances. The only other person that can handle a case like this and win would be Attorney Bria Lanai. I need to make sure that I call her tonight or first thing in the morning. The trials will be here before you know it.

"How long do you plan to stay?" Detective Evans asked as we pulled into the hospital's parking lot. I had to think about it because I hadn't given it any thought. I bought a one-way ticket. Hell, I didn't even make reservations at a hotel. I may have to get Kenna's keys and stay at her house if it gets too late. I do have the address. I just need the keys.

"I have no clue," I began responding. "I need to make sure that I file the proper paperwork needed to be guardian over Kenna and the baby for right now. That's one of my main concerns. I need to handle that before one of her parents gets wind and uses this situation to their advantage.

We arrived at the hospital. Detective Evans showed his credentials, and we were allowed access to where Kenna was being kept. She laid swollen yet peaceful. It didn't make sense unless you were right here looking at her for yourself. My eyes watered up thinking about her strength to endure all that she has, and she still continues to fight. She has not lost her faith or hope. I kneeled on the floor and held her hand. I cried and began praying and speaking with God.

Father God, I come to you humbly asking for your mercy for my friend Kenna and her baby. Father, I know I don't pray often, because I don't know how. I thought it was a specific way. To be totally honest, I also stopped praying because I was confused about religion. I didn't know what to believe, so I stopped believing. What I am about to say comes directly from my heart and a good place.

Father, Kenna may have struggled, but she continued holding on. She had that mustard seed of faith, whereas I didn't even have that. You know what she has endured because I know you had to be right by her side in order for her to come thus far. Father, download what she needs in her spirit to move forward and activate a miracle. You are the Miracle maker and Promise keeper. If it's in your will to perform a miracle on Kenna's life so that she can live a life of joy, Father I ask that you have your way.

Feed me your word also Father, I am ready to surrender. This load of life is too heavy for me to bare as well. Prepare me on a level of understanding so that when you feed me, I can feed others. Nurture and nourish me, Kenna, and baby Angel in our identity in you.

I need to ask you for a few more favors father. Help me to find Angel and heal Kenna. Expose who harmed Kenna, and last but not least, please Father, help me to throw all the evil doers in this entire fiasco in the pits of hell! I will be forever grateful! Father, I swear I will spread your name and share your true word with the world. Amen!

I stood up; I looked around Kenna's room to see if anything were left that could be used as evidence, as well as in Kenna's drawers. I was basically just looking for anything. I took her wallet and keys from her drawer and decided to keep them with me. I didn't want anyone stealing from her was my first thought. Secondly, I'm going to go stay at her house until she gets better. My mission is to find the baby, and make sure both Kenna and the baby are good before I feel comfortable going back. I felt light and with new hope. After we left Kenna's room, we visited the nursery, or babies room, I would call it. I was able to speak with the nurse on duty that particular night. She explained the exact same thing to me that she explained to Detective Evans, except for one fact, she noticed that the young man shook awfully bad like he had the beginning stages of Parkinson's disease. I looked at Detective Evans and said, "That had to be Mark, so I wonder where Marco is?" That question was left posed as we thanked her and headed out.

Once we left the hospital and got back to the detectives car, it dawned on me to have Detective Evans call the airport. So, I said, "Call the airport to see if there were two tickets bought under Marco Singfields name. If so, we need to find out if they were bought with two different departures from Ohio date's and if either were bought with a return date," I suggested.

Detective Evans called the airlines, low and behold, one ticket did have a return date and the other was one-way. The passenger was scheduled to return today.

"The plane departed forty-five minutes ago from Raleigh-Durham International," the Chief began. "It is scheduled to land in Ohio in one hour," he stated.

"Mark Singfield is wanted in an attempted murder and kidnapping, we are pretty damn sure that he is traveling with an accomplice who happens to be an elderly lady," Detective Evans stated. "Is it possible to come and view the airport security camera's? We are in the vicinity and want to see if we can identify Mark and his accomplice together, with the kidnapped baby?" Detective Evans asked.

The airport security Chief agreed to allow us access. "We are on our way!" Detective Evan's said. He turned his siren on and sped through traffic like he was on a chase. In the meantime, he called his superior and asked him to contact Zella Airlines in Ohio. The Captain contacted security at Zella and identified himself. He requested to speak with whomever was in charge of security. When the Airport top security Chief took the call, the Captain again identified himself and introduced Detective Evans into the call. Detective Evan's greeted the Chief and began by saying, "Chief, I need this request expedited. There is a man and possibly a woman who may be armed and dangerous with mental issues on flight 537 coming from Raleigh North Carolina heading to Ohio. The passenger is flying under the name Marco Singfield, but he is not really Marco. He is Marco's identical twin. His name is Mark. Mark Singfield is wanted for attempted murder and kidnapping. He was last seen with an accomplice in her early to mid-sixties. We need him detained on the plane. Be careful, a baby girl who is days old was kidnapped by the two."

"Do not allow anyone off that plane! I will send the best pictures that we have as of now in order to ID them. Give me a fax or phone number. Both are considered dangerous and could have weapons on them. I am en route to Raleigh International to view their camera's. I will contact you if I have any further updates. If you receive any, please contact me on this number," Detective Evans began. "Until then, when that plane lands, and they are captured, I need to be the first to know. Again, my name is Detective Evans. I just received your fax number. I will be sending over the pictures and any other pertinent information," he stated.

We went straight to the security office once we arrived at Raleigh International. Detective Evans identified himself. Security was able to show recordings of Mark coming in and pacing around in line. He had the baby, and the lady accomplice is with him.

Detective Evans immediately called the Chief back and told him that all parties boarded the plane. "We are at Raleigh International watching the footage," Detective Evans stated.

"They are just about to land," the airport Chief began responding. "We have security in place. I will personally call you back when they are apprehended," he said.

Detective Evans and I thanked everyone for their cooperation and exited the airport heading back to his car. Once we entered his car, we both wanted to breathe a sigh of relief, but it was a little too early. I silently said, "Thank you father!" He took me back to my rental car and told me that he would keep me posted. I thanked him, jumped in my rental, and headed to Kenna's.

It didn't take me long using my G.P.S. to find her beautiful home. The neighborhood was breath taking. I walked into the home and almost had a heart attack. Marco was hogged tied and laying on the floor. He wasn't dead. Blood covered his nose and there was blood on his head. I called Detective Evans and explained what I walked into. I gave him Kenna's address and he arrived there in record time. He also called for backup and a paramedic. They all pulled up at almost the exact same time. I opened the door to allow them access.

The Paramedic worked on Marco and was able to get him up and on a stretcher. Marco was discombobulated at first. Detective Evan's and the other officer asked Marco a barrage of questions that he answered to the best of his ability. There was something he said that caught my attention and pissed me off! I had to catch myself. Marco told Detective Evans that the lady traveling with Mark as his accomplice is their grandmother. She is his mother's mother. His mother contacted her while in prison and promised to split some of Marks inheritance with her if she got rid of Kenna and him. Mrs. Singfield lied to her mother and told her that Marco was going against the family and that Kenna, and he together had her framed. Mrs. Singfield wanted her mother to keep Kenna's baby and go into hiding until she is released. She claimed it's the little girl that she's always wanted to have, but never could.

Before I could tell Marco that he and I share the same evil lying scandalous mother, Detective Evans got the call for which we were awaiting. It wasn't the news that we were expecting.

"Hello Detective Evans," the Chief began. "Baby Angel was rescued, and she is safe. Mark and the elderly lady put up a fight. Mark, during the tussle with the police, was able to grab a gun from one of the officers holsters. Mark is a big strong guy," the Chief stated. "He was able to strong arm an officer and shot him in his chest. The other officers began firing on Mark and killed him. The elderly woman is in custody and is en route to the Police Department," he stated.

"Thank you Chief," Detective Evans began. "We will make sure that we have her expedited back here first thing in the morning, and someone will be there to escort the baby back. It may be Attorney Body," he said as he looked at me and smiled. "I will contact you first thing in the morning with all the details," he stated.

"No problem," the Chief responded.

Marco was loaded up and transported to the hospital for observations. I wanted to go with him, but I couldn't. I was exhausted. I decided to tidy up, make sure that there was no blood drippings anywhere, take a shower and hit Kenna's bed. I may be on a plane early going to get baby Angel.

Chapter Nineteen

Born Again

I took a nice hot shower and laid across Kenna's bed. I began doing something that was out of the normal for me. I began saying a prayer.

Father God, I want your love, mercy, and faithfulness to continue to cover me daily. This way, I will not fear whatever comes against me. I am learning to trust you Lord. This I didn't do before, like Kenna. Father, please continue to breathe life into Kenna and thank you for returning baby Angel. Amen.

I passed out cold from exhaustion.

I awoke to my phone ringing; it was Detective Evans. "Good Morning sleepy head," he said.

"Good Morning Evans," I responded. He laughed like I had honestly said something funny.

"Oh, it's Evans now, huh?"

"Well, what's your first name?" I asked.

"It's Calvin, what's yours Miss Body?" he responded.

"Well, Good Morning Calvin, my name is Charmaine," I said. "What's going on?" I asked.

"Well," he began. "You have a flight leaving out at eleven a.m. back to Ohio to pick up Baby Angel. It will be a round trip flight. You will need to be back at the airport at four p.m. to return. Can you handle that?" he asked.

"Yes I can," I stated.

"Good, I will swing by to pick you up at nine thirty."

"Okay, I will be ready," I responded.

I jumped up and showered. I threw on a cute little Nike outfit and my tennis shoes. I put my hair in a ponytail, put on my baseball cap and I was ready to go. I made a cup of coffee while I waited for Calvin to pull up. He pulled up in his personal car. I ran out after securing the house, to greet him. We rolled by Wendy's grabbed a breakfast sandwich and headed to the airport. We laughed and talked like old friends until we arrived at the airport for my departure. Calvin stayed with me until I boarded the plane and made me promise to contact him once I landed in Ohio.

I slept the entire flight back and headed straight to CPS where they were holding baby Angel. I went through the security check in order to validate who I was. She was the most beautiful baby girl I had ever seen. I called Calvin and told him that I had her. We talked on the phone until I arrived back at the airport in Ohio, returning to Raleigh. I didn't even have time to go check on my house or anything.

We boarded our return flight after going through security and arrived back in Raleigh where Calvin was en route to pick us up. He said that he was five minutes away. I decided to call Attorney Bria Lanai to fill her in on what was going on. She was floored and welcomed the case. I gave her access to my security codes on my computer and the pass code to my cabinet so that she would have access to all of the information. I promised to forward her anything else that would be helpful from here. She thanked me and we both promised to stay connected.

Calvin pulled up right when I hung up the line. I was happy to see him. He lit up when he saw how beautiful baby Angel was. "Where to," he asked.

"Let's get this baby reacquainted with her mother," I stated.

We headed straight to the hospital. We walked in Kenna's room, and she still laid in bed as though she was in a peaceful state resting. I began praying to God that baby Angel breathes life back into Kenna. I laid her on Kenna's chest and asked God to do his magic. At first baby Angel laid peacefully sleeping on her mother's chest. Calvin and I watched on as baby Angel began squirming around and started making a little whimper sound. We stood in witness as Kenna reached around and began rubbing her back to comfort her. She held on to her as though she knew that Angel was placed there.

I began getting choked up and crying. "Fight Kenna, fight." I prayed through tears I could no longer control. "Fight girl, your baby needs you! Wake up Kenna, please wake up! This is not the end, it is a new beginning, a new life. You have been born again, fight," I continued saying. Calvin was getting as choked up as I was. He whispered that he was going to go and check on Marco. He was still in the hospital being treated. I said okay as he exited the room.

I sat next to Kenna's bed and began praying.

Father, I beg for you to deliver Kenna. There is no healing too hard for you. Please bless her with your love, renew her in strength, and heal her internally and externally. In your name Father. Thank you in advance! Amen.

I sat back in the chair and waited. I decided to hit Calvin's phone up in order to check on Marco. He said that he arrived right on time, Marco was being released. They were discussing some of what transpired while they waited on Marco's release papers, and they would be down in a few minutes.

I began humming Jesus loves me and noticed Kenna trying to wake up. I saw her head toss back and forth. She also began rubbing on Angel again. Twenty minutes or so passed and Marco walked in the room with Calvin. He rushed over to Kenna and the baby and hugged them both. He began talking to Kenna through tears and pain.

"Kenna, I am so sorry, I would never in any life hurt you. I love you too much for that. I have always loved you! I will never speak to mother again; she can rot in hell! Her greed and sadistic ways has caused so many people pain. Kenna, to be honest, I found out about Mark when I was younger. I hated the guy although he was my brother and we looked exactly alike. He was mean spirited, like mother. It didn't help that he had mental issues. Between he and mother, they caused me to have issues myself. I am going to seek help for my issues, I promise you!"

We all were in tears as he laid his head on Kenna's shoulders and begged her to wake up. "I love you Kenna, please don't leave me. I never got to give you the ring I bought you. I want to marry you and make you my wife. I love Angel also, she is beautiful just like you," Marco stated.

"I love you and baby Angel," Kenna said as plain as day to Marco! We all jumped up and began hugging one another. We cried and thanked our heavenly father! Calvin went to the nurses station to get a doctor to come in and check Kenna out. Baby Angel began crying herself. Marco picked her up and began walking and patting her back gently. He sat down on the love seat when she continued to cry and retrieved a diaper, wipes, and her bottle. Baby Angel also had a couple of receiving blankets in her bag. Marco used one to lay her on as he changed her diaper. He fed and burped her and wrapped her back up nicely and snuggly laying her back on her mother.

Chapter Twenty

Fruition
Two Months Later

I have been home now for two months. Marco left Ohio and moved in with me, we are doing great. Mr. Singfield bought a home in North Carolina and visits us often. He even purchased this house for me and Marco as an early wedding gift. We are engaged and we are both in high school. Charmaine watches Angel during the day and works from home mostly. If she have a hearing or has to make a run, Mr. Singfield babysits. He adores her.

Attorney Body went back to Ohio and recused herself from the case, sold her practice to Attorney Bria Lanai and moved to North Carolina to be closer to Calvin. Baby Angel is the love of all of our lives. She has taught us so much about real love. I kept to my word, I visit Candies son often and have built a repour with the staff. I also began filing the proper paperwork to gain custody of him. He is so excited.

We have trial in two days. I can't wait! Mrs. Singfield is up first, second will be the Bishop and the Assistant Bishop. The last will be First Lady. Mr. Singfield will watch Angel as we head to Ohio tomorrow. Hopefully, we won't be there longer than a few days.

Tonight, we decided to have a nice peaceful and relaxing night. We are already packed and ready to go. Calvin and Charmain stopped by on their way home from dinner. They seem to really care for one another. We laughed, talked, and prayed. Charmain was a little distant tonight. It just seemed like she was struggling with something and just didn't know to release it. So, as we prayed, I asked God to release within her, her issues. This way we could all talk about it and possibly help her.

"Charmain, I feel the weight that you're carrying. Please release it," I asked with sincerity. Charmain looked at us all as everyone reiterated my request.

"I want to say something, but I fear opening up old wounds," Charmain said.

"Charmain, we all are working on healing," Marco began. "Through therapy, I am discovering that I don't really know who I am, and it's okay. I am rebuilding a new and better me. We cannot continue to allow our parents burdens to affect our growth," Marco continued saying.

"You're right Marco, I would like to share my story with the people that I love. I started to tell Kenna some of my story over the phone. I never finished. I found out that I was adopted at an early age. My mother got pregnant at fourteen years old by a church member who abused her, pimped her out as well as allowed her to be molested frequently. She gave me away and stayed with the church member and continued prostituting. The family that she gave me to was the best family in the world. I was shown a lot of love and support. They were always honest with me about my biological mother. I would see her in church, and she would act as though she didn't know who I was. At first it hurt; the pain quickly vanished. I didn't understand any of my life until I met you Kenna," Charmain said.

"Me, why me?" I asked. Charmain took several deep breaths as everyone looked in her direction awaiting her reply.

"Caroline Campbell-Singfield is my biological mother and Bishop Charles is my biological father. My real name is Charmaine Campbell-Body." Marco's mouth dropped, and I wanted to let out a scream but couldn't find it. "When Mr. Singfield came to my office after you left Kenna, he was traumatized. He found my original birth certificate tucked away with two more birth certificates. Caroline lied to us all," she began. Marco wore a look of frustration, yet empathy for Charmain.

"So, you are my sister?" he asked.

"Yes, I am you and Marks biological sister," Charmain replied.

There was a knock at the door that startled us all. Marco and Calvin both went to see who it was. While they were away, I gave Charmain a hug and told her how proud I was of her. She was doing a wonderful job. We heard the men returning with Marco's dad Mr. Singfield. He was heading home and saw all the cars and decided to stop.

"You are right on time dad," Marco began. Baby Angel had awaken, so Marco jumped up to get her. He brought out a diaper and her wipes, and I went to the kitchen to get her a bottle because she was hungry.

"Would you like a cold beverage or some coffee or anything Mr. Singfield," I asked.

"No, thank you doll. I just left from having some super over my friend Ms. Agnes's house. That woman know she can cook." We all laughed and were incredibly happy that dad had a friend who helped look after him.

"Okay, where was I?" Charmaine asked. "You were at the point where you discovered that you were my biological sister," Marco stated. Mr. Singfields eye's got filled with tears. Marco got up and moved next to him and hugged him. It's okay dad. In order for us to heal, we have to face the truth no matter what it is. God will give us the strength we need, right?"

Mr. Singfield wiped his eye's and said, "You're right son. Son, I found out a lot of stuff about your mother I didn't know. Some stuff I did know but chose to ignore because I loved her. I was shocked when your momma told me she was pregnant with twins. That was because I couldn't have any kids. I accepted you and Mark as my own," Mr. Singfield began.

"WHAT!?" Marco screamed.

"No son, you're not my biological son. When you and Mark were babies, it was a lot for me to care for another man's children. Especially a set of identical twins. Caroline was never there to help, and I was losing it. My sister was great with kids and asked me to send Mark to her. Mark had Schizophrenia, Obsessive Compulsive Disorder, and Borderline Personality Disorder. As Mark grew up, he became too much of a responsibility for my sister to handle. She was able to afford to put him in a Mental Asylum that genuinely cared for him. When my sister passed away, she left a lot of money for his caretakers.

Caroline decided then and only then that she wanted to be a piece of a mother and a caretaker. She took it upon herself behind my back to visit him and tell him who she really was. He had no previous memory of her or knowledge. She showed him baby pictures of him along with her that were really you and her. She had him moved from one place to another and would buy him in order for him to like her. One day, she thought it was a bright idea to bring him to meet you Marco, his identical twin he had no previous knowledge of. That didn't go over as planned. Neither of you liked one another, but Mark remembered where we stayed and would come there when he would see you leave or if he wanted to be ornery he would come and agitate you." Mr. Singfield said.

"Do you know who my biological father is?" Marco asked.

"Yes, Assistant Bishop Larry Brown. He is the First Ladies brother," Mr. Singfield responded.

None of this sounds right. This entire fiasco is sick. He rapped me, The Bishop and First lady rapped and pimped me out along with my parents. My daughter is my fiancé's step niece. This makes no sense...

Chapter Twenty-One

Court Is In Session

I have waited for this day for so long. "All Rise for Judge James Grafton." We all stood in respect for the judges entrance. I had butterflies in my stomach as the attorney's took to the floor with their opening arguments. Attorney Bia Lanai is a beast! She came out of the gates calling the shots. She had a team with her who were organized and as diligent as she appeared.

She called several of the young ladies who were molested to the stand, she cross examined Caroline, the Assistant Bishop, First Lady, my father, and my mother along with a few of the Deacons. She had me, and Marco testify last. We ate their behinds up!

We adjourned for recess while the jury made its ruling. They called us back in the courtroom in less than two hours.

"Bishop Charles Brackston, Theresa Brown-Brackston, Caroline Campbell-Singfield, do you have any last words before we read the verdict?"

They all said, "No," your honor.

The jury began reading the charges and the counts. The Bishop received life in a federal prison. First Lady received twenty-five years in a federal prison. Caroline received thirty years in a federal prison, the Assistant Bishop and my father received ten years each. My mother, and Deacon Ladson got less time because they turned state's evidence. They received five years apiece.

I was ecstatic! I was satisfied with everything. We left the courtroom feeling like we accomplished a lot.

We went out to dinner to celebrate. Afterward we went back to the hotel to finally relax and pray. Thank you Father is all I kept saying!! Marco and I headed back to our hotel room and so did Charmain and

Calvin. We made love for the first time, and it was the best experience in the world. I felt free.

Marco rolled over to call and check on Mr. Singfield and Angel. He also wanted to let him know how we made out in court. I picked my phone up to call CPS about Candies son. I wanted to let him know that I will still be able to come and pick him up this week. I thought we wouldn't be back in time. We assumed that we would be here for several days, but it turns out we can fly out of here first thing in the morning.

Marco allowed the phone to ring several times, there was no answer. "Maybe he is over Ms. Agnes's house," he thought out loud. "I will give him a few minutes. Dad maybe doing something and just don't have the phone near him."

Marco called back about thirty minutes later and said, "Hello."

The person on the other end said, "Hello Marco."

"May I speak to my father?" Marco asked.

The lady laughed a sinister laugh and said, "He is tied up at the moment." Marco looked at the phone as though he didn't understand what she said. I could hear her voice through the phone.

"May I ask who I'm speaking with?" Marco said.

"You don't recognize my voice," she asked.

"No," he said.

"This is your grandmother, your mothers mother. I came to get Angel."

My life is God's plan. I am learning to understand that a part of his plan for my life requires me to use my gift of Godly discernment with free will. Free will reveals itself in decision making. God's intent for our lives, not just my own, is to arm us with not only free will, but the ability to carry out his decree. No one knows the objective but God. I've struggled most of my life with the interpretation of the word, so I am learning to go to God directly and ask for understanding. God is highly exalted above all things. His moral perfection stands in contrast to evil people. My studies have shown me that God overrules the natural order to accomplish an act that people may or may not have requested. I am also learning that we can assume that we understand what is needed, expect God to agree, and answer our prayers in that way. God has options outside of natural order. With that being said, I have to stop exposing my wounds to the world. I need to adjust to my growth in peace and not continue exposing my troubles to my adversaries.

I've wasted a lot of valuable time while going through my trials. My focus was on the wrong thing. I was focused more on being stabbed in the back, than I was on the hand that held the knife. In the end, I had to learn how to forgive those who purposefully harmed me. Just as I am learning that in order for me to ascend to my next level of understanding, forgiveness is key. I will benefit from their betrayal, and the Creator will take the things used to assassinate my character to create a better version of me. I will absorb the blows, tally them up, and glorify them off.

A part of my process has allowed me to understand that no one truly knows the truth outside of the Creator. The Bible is really a theological and a literacy mosaic. The meaning of all the pieces is found in the completed mosaic. Don't get this misconstrued, the pattern isn't often clear. A mosaic isn't imposed on the pieces; it derives from them. People will continue to speculate, form their own opinions, and pass down generational myths that will have us all discombobulated.

In A.D. 301-304, the Roman Emperor Diocletian burned and had burned thousands of copies of the Bible. Thousands of years later, copies that survived were altered significantly, books were removed, and other books were disregarded and considered not divine scripture. According to the deciding Council, they were of no authority in the church of God. Manuscripts of the New Testament books were lost or destroyed, and the original Bible was never found. Most are aware that there are connections between the testaments that can't be coincidental. I go straight to the Creator to validate what his true word is whenever I'm in search of the truth. I've always had an issue with Council determining what was actually prophesied and what wasn't.

Moving forward, my main objective as of right now is to stop looking in the rearview of who I used to be. I believe that I was fearful and wonderfully made. God expects me to elevate my perspective in order to transform me on my next level. My journey is my own, yet he walks with me. He has not forsaken me, it's time for me to pick up the pieces and deal with my current issue at hand. I had a private moment with my Father, and I trust at the core of this traumatic experience; God will make a way out of no way. I refuse to be emotionally bound when I am spiritually free.

Chapter Twenty-Two

What Wasn't Foreseen?

L

eaving Angel in the care of Mr. Singfield was a no-brainer, he loved her. None of us could have foresaw anyone causing her or him any harm. I am determined like no other to get her back safely and to make sure that Mr. Singfield is safe as well. I felt horrible for both of them and even worse for not being in the immediate vicinity and able to help. We left the trial feeling hopeful and somewhat relieved. I am steadfast in getting my baby back and ending this joyless rollercoaster ride.

As I listened to Marco begging his grandmother not to harm his father and Angel, I was already packing my clothing in my suitcase, and calling the airlines to book a one-way flight to return home. Once I was able to book an emergency flight back, I called Charmaine and Calvin to explain what was going on. I also informed them that I've already booked our flight out. Charmaine was visibly frustrated and upset. She filled Calvin in on everything that had transpired. Calvin immediately jumped on his phone and called his Captain, Captain St. Clair. Calvin filled him in on everything and asked that this situation be expedited and treated with V.I.P. status. He requested that Special Units drop everything immediately and treat this situation as though the President of the United States had been kidnapped. There will be no sirens blaring upon arrival. Move in with speed and precision. There was no room for error or allowing time for Marco and Charmaine's grandmother to flee. This move was to be swift and calculated.

Charmaine and Calvin booked flights out as well. They were able to get a private flight out due to Calvin's position on the force and due to the respect he and Captain St. Clair held for one another. This allowed them to arrive a little before me and Marco.

Surprisingly, Marco and Charmaine's grandmother put up a heck of a fight. The Special Units team had to call in a negotiator to try and reason or delay time, whichever worked first. The grandmother refused to comply with Special Units or the negotiator. Unbeknown to her, they were scaling the home, and entered through an upstairs window in order to subdue the situation. Time was not their friend. The smell of gasoline was heavy. One light of a match and the entire place would be in flames. They couldn't allow the grandmother an opportunity to hurt Mr. Singfield or harm Angel. Once she realized that she was cornered with no options, she swung around pointing her gun in one hand, and a lit candle in another. God had to be amongst us because the smell of gasoline alone was intensely strong. Her hands shook with fear, making it impossible for her to hit her mark with a bullet. She was unable to think clearly enough, thankfully, to drop the lit candle. She was purposely distracted as one officer grabbed her hands, and another moved in swiftly to grab the gun and the lit candle. She was able to shoot off one shot before she was tackled and cuffed by her wrist and ankles, then hauled off to jail.

Mr. Singfield and Angel were transported to the nearest hospital and checked out before being released to go home. Ms. Agnes demanded that Marco's dad come and stay with her. She stated in a matter-of-fact way, "I dare the old bat to come my way!" We all laughed but she was not playing. Mr. Singfield was given ointment for his wrist abrasions, after x-rays were taken to make sure there wasn't any underlying damage. He and Ms. Agnes exited the hospital promising to check in later. Angel was fine, but hungry and definitely wet. I had to thank God for covering this entire situation. Things could have definitely went in the opposite direction.

We all thanked Calvin and decided that we would relax today, and maybe catch up in a day or so to have dinner. As Marco and I headed home, we both began giving thanks. I laid my head back on the headrest and began speaking with God as though no one else existed.

"Father, I would like to thank you for protecting our loved ones. I surrender to you. I no longer feel like I have to be the one to protect myself from going through tough times. I am still trying to master forgiveness. Every time I try to grasp a hold of the forgiving concept, I'm left feeling drained and empty, maybe it's not the concept I need to grasp. Do you feel like that Father when we don't obey you? Do you really forgive us of our debts and transgressions blotting out our sins? Strengthen me where I am weak Lord! I feel as though you will not allow me to fully understand the refreshing, until I am able to move forward on your word with Godly discernment."

"I want to live without consequence and trust you to always protect me. Cover me Father, healing my pain and my wounds." I took a moment and paused in thought before proceeding forward. *"I vow beginning today Father, that I will try harder to walk in forgiveness. Forgiveness, I am learning, is not about the other person, and the harm or pain they've caused me. It's about releasing me from carrying the weight. I got it Father; I think I truly got it this time. Thank you, Amen!"*

Marco looked over at me and said, "Amen," as well.

"We have a lot of work to do Marco," I began. "In order to do this the right way, we have to know and understand what is right," I stated.

"I agree," Marco responded. "Leaning on our own understanding has gotten us nowhere," I continued.

I was ecstatic when we finally pulled in the driveway. We hurried in and tended to Angel first. I gave her a nice bath, fresh pajamas, and a nice warm bottle. Marco checked the perimeter of the house. It took him a little longer than normal before he turned on the alarm system and laid across the bed. He was a little quiet, but I didn't want to think anything about it.

Angel must have been exhausted. She didn't even finish her formula before drifting off into a deep sleep. Marco got up without saying a word, took her to her bed and returned. We laid across our bed in complete silence. I thought about the steps we needed to work on in order to grow our faith moving forward.

Marco posed a question that I wasn't really prepared to answer. "Kenna," he began. "If we are working on forgiveness, does that mean that we have to forgive everyone?" he asked. I sat and thought about his question. I wanted to make sure that I answered him honestly.

"Yes, I think it does mean that. We need to forgive wholeheartedly and mean it. I think we should continue to seek God's strength in order to help us do it and mean it. We can then one day go to everyone and tell them that we forgive them. As of right now Marco, I am not ready." Marco lay on his back with his hands under his head. He looked around at nothing.

"Marco, I do have one condition that I need to speak to God about," I said. He looked at me like I was a nutcase.

"What's that?" he finally asked with a questioning look on his face.

"I will forgive them in God's name, but does that mean I have to deal with them? I am on the struggle bus," I said laughingly.

Marco smiled before grabbing me and planting a kiss on my lips. I kissed him back and cuddled up under him for a good night's rest.

Chapter Twenty-Three

New Journey

Marco and I awoke rejuvenated. Angel had awakened and just laid in her bed cooing and smiling. "Good morning sunshine," I said as I picked Angel up to smother her with kisses. I took her into the living area, changed her diaper and headed off into the kitchen to fix her a bottle. Marco finally came out of the bathroom, kissed me on the cheek, and went to play with Angel. "What would you like for breakfast?" I asked him. Marco was so busy coo-cooing that he hadn't heard a word I said. I laughed because he looked like a big kid playing with a baby doll. "Mr. Marco, would you like a hot breakfast or cereal sir?" I asked.

"Babe, I will eat some cereal. No need in fixing anything, I can do it," he said. I made him a hot breakfast anyway. He needed to eat, and I was going to make sure that I did everything a good girlfriend would do, even though we are not official.

"Your mommy is in the kitchen fixing daddy some breakfast my Angel. Daddy needs to go and set the table. I will be back to give you all the attention you want," Marco said in baby talk to Angel as he made his way into the kitchen. Marco set the table and sat down to take a sip of his juice as his phone began ringing. "Hello," Marco began. "Really," he said in a concerned voice. "Okay, I will meet you there," he responded. Marco hung up the phone and began explaining that his father was having chest pain. Ms. Agnes called the paramedic, and they are transporting him over to the hospital for observation."

"I will keep him in my prayers," I said. I made Marco a bacon sandwich while he ran into the room to put his shoes and sweat jacket on. I handed him his sandwich and a few napkins as he re-entered the kitchen to kiss me before he left. "I will call you with any updates," he said. He kissed Angel and left right out.

I sat down for a minute just to relax my mind. I had a list of things to do in preparation for the week. School was starting, and I needed to get our laundry done. It was also important to me that Marco and I started this week out on a more positive note.

As I busied myself around the house taking advantage of Angel's nap time, my phone began ringing. The caller ID came up Charmaine Body. "Hello Charmaine," I answered with joy in my voice.

"Hey girl," she began responding. "How are you?" she asked. I didn't want to begin the conversation with anything draining, but I needed to tell her about Mr. Singfield having to go to the hospital.

"I'm doing great. I am just waiting for Marco to call me and let me know how his dad is doing," I began saying.

"What happened to his dad?" Charmaine inquired.

"Ms. Agnes called us this morning and said that he was having chest pain. She called an ambulance to have him taken into the hospital. Marco met them over there. I stayed back so that I could get some things done around here. You know like I know; it has been one thing after another," I stated. Charmaine was quiet for a brief minute before saying,

"Well, you know that Calvin and I will definitely keep him in our prayers," Charmaine finally responded, sounding irritated, which was odd.

"So, what else is going on?" I asked.

"Kenna, I hate to even mention it now that you've told me about Mr. Singfield," Charmaine began. "But Calvin received a call from the jail. I guess our grandmother got into an argument and a scuffle with a girl who was locked up in her same pod. The argument got violent and out of control. Supposedly, you and your parents were brought up. According to some of the inmates who witnessed the altercation, they were playing cards in the rec room, and an argument broke out. Evidently, the girl knew grandmother and mentioned Marco's and my mother by name. She began slandering our mother, and claiming in front of the others, that she should be ashamed of herself for taking part in cult activities and misrepresenting the Lord. This set grandmother off. She began yelling, "You don't know what you're talking about." I guess the girl responded with, "The heck if I don't! My son is Kenna's brother. I had an affair with ole Deacon Ricks and beat him and his wife's, behind. The wife tried to get me back by having me investigated for child abuse and abandonment. You know exactly who I'm talking about! Your grandson is in love with my man's daughter, Kenna, and there is nothing you can do about it!" the girl was heard saying.

"Grandmother, in a rage, pulled out a shank and they began tussling. That's when grandmother stabbed her in her stomach and in her chest. Before she fell over, the girl stabbed out at grandmother and the shank pierced her heart. They both are dead," Charmaine explained, sounding pitiful. She almost made me feel bad. I would have assumed, if I didn't know any better, that her and her grandmother had a great relationship.

I was quiet for a minute. I needed to wrap my head around all of this. Candie's son is in the system, my brother is in the system, Marco and I are starting school, I already have a baby, how am I going to handle all of this? Although I thought it, I had no idea that I spoke out loud until Charmaine responded. "Let me talk to Calvin. If it's meant to work out, God will make a way for it all to work out," she stated before my line clicked with another call.

"Okay Charmaine, can you come by later if you're not busy?" I asked quickly before clicking over to the other line.

"Okay," Charmaine began responding. I have some business to take care of first, I will try to come afterward."

Chapter Twenty-Four

Back in Rotation

"H

ello," I said, sounding exhausted.

"Hey babe, what's wrong?" Marco asked.

"We will talk when you come home, babe. What's more important right now is how your dad is?" I asked.

"Okay honey, uhm dad's doing okay. They are going to keep him overnight for further observation. The only information that they have been able to provide as of now is the fact that he didn't have a heart attack and he hasn't had a stroke. Which is formidable information," Marco stated.

"That is a blessing," I responded.

"Yes, it is. I should be leaving here in about five minutes. Do you need anything while I am out?" Marco asked.

"No babe, I am good. Thanks!" I responded.

"Okay, I am on my way. Love you!"

As the line clicked, I mumbled, "I love you more.

I decided to start dinner while putting a load in the washing machine. This was some fried chicken, mashed potatoes, baked broccoli type of day. I was able to wash, clean and season my chicken before Angel woke up screaming for attention. "Awe mommy's Angel is really mad," I said in baby talk back to her. "It's okay sweetie, mommy's right here," I said. I picked Angel up and checked her diaper. She'd used it outside of her diaper. She must have a stomachache. The way she was crying was telling me that she doesn't feel well. I removed the diaper and cleaned her up enough to take her into my bathroom to bathe her in the sink. I gave her a nice lavender bath, fed her, and put her in her swing so that I could clean up the mess I had just made trying to get her clean. Once I was able to get everything together, I put the washed load in the drier, adding a load to the washer, before I was able to get back in the living area and collapse.

"Hey babe," Marco said as he walked in the house.

"Hello Hun," I responded back.

"What's up?" he asked.

"What's not up?" I answered back as I slouched down on the couch looking defeated. Marco laughed as he leaned over and lightly pushed Angel's swing and rewound the music. I caught him up on the last thirty minutes of my day, saving what Charmaine had confided in until we both relaxed for a little while. "I will finish the cooking. Relax, I got this," Marco said.

Marco headed into the kitchen and began doing his thing before he turned and asked, "Hey babe, what news did Charmaine call with?" I heard him when he asked but wanted to deliver the message with sincerity when it came to his grandmother and not appear nonchalant. Marco left the kitchen and walked into the living area where I sat, and he re-asked his question.

I turned toward Marco and began, "Charmaine called and said that Calvin received a call from the jail. Your grandmother got into an altercation with an inmate. From what I gather, it was the young lady my father had his affair with. I'm not sure if you remember me telling you how a lady came to the house with a child she stated was my father's?" I asked Marco.

"Yes," Marco responded, sounding leery.

"According to the witness statements a card game ensued. Someone mentioned your mother, you, and Charmaine's names, along with my parents, the Bishop, and First Lady. They basically argued about the case. Your grandmother was set off when it was said that her daughter was involved in cult activities. She claimed the inmate had no knowledge of the truth. The argument escalated worse when the inmate claimed that her son was my brother, and the fact that you and I were together. The mere mention of my name took it to the next level. Your grandmother pulled out a shank and they tussled. Your grandmother allegedly stabbed the young lady in her stomach and in her chest. Before the young lady fell over, she stabbed your grandmother in her heart. They both are dead," I said, feeling bad for Charmaine, Marco, and my little brother.

"Wow," Marco began. "I wonder if they've contacted our mother. She is our grandmothers next of kin outside of myself and Charmaine," he continued.

"Honey, Charmaine is going to speak with Calvin to see if she has been, or if there is any possible way she could be told," I said. Marco sat staring off into space. He really didn't have much to say after that. He returned to the kitchen to finish cooking dinner. I was beginning to worry about him. With so much going on in our lives, it feels like we are on an unending cycle. He hasn't been seen for his depression since he has officially moved here. I think it's time he sought professional help before he snaps. I will bring it up to him later, I thought.

While Angel was still asleep, I tried to finish the laundry. I wanted to slip off into the bathroom while Marco was busy in order to have a little private time with God. Once I entered the restroom, I was able to exhale. I got on bended knees in front of the bathroom sink and began thanking God for my sanity first and foremost. I get emotional at the thought of not technically being an adult but being put in the position due to life's circumstances. *Father, please give me clarity. I want to listen like your son. I want to show up in this family as what you have spoken over my life. I don't want to continue showing up for my family as sin. I cannot allow my insecurities to show up as who I am connected to. Father, I do not want to be the creation that disrespects the creator because I am afraid to embrace who I am. I need your help... Amen!*

I re-entered the living area just as Marco was finishing dinner. I picked up on the tail end of a conversation he was having with his dad, Mr. Singfield. "Okay dad, I will update you as soon as I hear anything else. I am glad to hear you are doing well. I love you more," Marco stated as he hung up his line. "Honey," I began. "We need to call Charmaine and see if she can watch Angel on Monday, you know school starts. I will also see if Calvin had time to get that information for you all also," I stated.

Marco sat next to me, he leaned forward and began shaking. "Marco honey, are you okay?" I asked. He said nothing. I rubbed his back trying to get him to relax his mind and body. A few minutes passed before he even noticed that I was sitting next to him. He looked over at me as though he was shocked to see me there. "Honey, we need to find you a doctor here in town. What do you think about that?" I asked. Marco said nothing. I got up and headed over to the table to eat the dinner that he prepared. It was delicious. Marco came over and joined me without saying a word. After we both finished eating, I stood and began cleaning up and washing our dishes. I decided to call Charmaine once more. I needed advice. Marco was beginning to make me feel a little uneasy.

"Hello Charmaine, how are you holding up?" I asked. "I'm good. Calvin is planning for you, Marco, and I to visit the prison. He is downtown speaking with the Captain. Hopefully, he should be contacting me back soon," she stated. "That sounds great. Charmaine, I need to talk to you about Marco. He's acting strange and began shaking and acting quite differently. His behavior is concerning because he reminds me of Mark and how he acted. Not only that, but we start school on Monday," I continued. "With everything that has transpired, I forgot to mention that I have a hearing for custody of Candie's son coming up soon."

"Marco has to get it together, or I will not have a chance of gaining custody of him or my little brother," I said.

"Wow, this is a lot going on," Charmaine began. "Well, I will take care of Angel while you are in school, and I will take you to court and maybe Mr. Singfield can watch her that day. I will also help you find Marco a doctor because it definitely sounds like he needs to be seen. I need you and Marco to do one thing for me though," Charmaine said with concern in her voice.

"Anything," I responded.

"Calvin and I were invited by his captain to attend his church tomorrow. It is a Non-Denominational Church. He stated that his Pastor is truly ordained and gifted. Both of you need to come and go with us. Maybe going to church again will help alleviate some of this stress and negativity going on.

"Yes, count us in," I said.

"Good, you two will be ready at 10:30 in the morning, we will be there to get you. We can then continue this discussion," Charmaine said with love.

"Thank you!" I responded as I hung up the line feeling relieved and hopeful.

Chapter Twenty-Five

Speak God

Marco and I prepared ourselves for church. It had been a long time since either he or I attended church. Seeing that I was starting anew, I wanted to give going to church and feeling the holy spirit within myself, in a church, another opportunity.

Marco seemed to be doing better so far today. He was excited about going to church with me and Angel. He jumped up before I did and took a shower so that he could help get Angel ready. With no signs of his previous behavior.

Before we knew it, time had flown past, and it was time for Calvin and Charmaine to pick us up. As I re-checked to make sure we had everything we needed, we heard the horn blow.

Church was a short drive away. We arrived and were shocked to see such a small church. We were greeted at the door by the Pastor and a greeting committee. They welcomed us with open arms. We've never felt this in any church. Once we entered the sanctuary, I felt a strong spiritual presence. I smiled as tears formed in my eyes. I looked over at Marco and saw that he was having the same experience. We took our seats as the choir ascended the choir stand. "All rise," Pastor Benedick requested. We all stood to our feet as the choir began singing, "Way maker, miracle worker, promise keeper..." The voices were angelic and filled with love. A few more songs were sung before a beautiful young woman stepped up to the podium and said, "Praise the Lord, everyone." The congregation repeated," Praise the Lord." She smiled and said, "Y'all didn't say it like you were here to praise anyone, let alone our Lord. I SAID PRAISE THE LORD!" she yelled in an effective way. Everyone began saying it with more meaning and emphasis. "Yes, hallelujah," she began shouting. The drums beat to a holy beat as people danced around in the holy spirit. After a few minutes, it all came to a halt. The beautiful woman identified herself as Ms. Baker. She gave church announcements, a financial report, and a brief summarization of what was going on in the church this month. Ms. Baker also gave a contact person's name out for any member in need of help, emergency assistance, counseling or in need of prayer.

Pastor Benedick soon entered the pulpit. He appeared to be in his mid-forties. He looked almost identical to Kofi Siriboe, who played Ralph Angel on Queen Sugar. "Let the church say Amen." He stood and looked around at the congregation as though he was deep in thought.

"Congregation, let me ask some of you a question. Do you know the Lord?" Pastor Benedick peered around at the congregation awaiting more than a few grumbles and "yes" shouts. "I'll ask my question again for those of you who are unsure of what I asked. Do you know the Lord?" the Pastor asked once again. "Let me say this," he began. "I'm about to take some of y'all to school up here today. Some of you devoted, so-called Christian folk, show up here on Sunday, and don't talk to God no more until the next Sunday. We need to learn how to partner with God every day. God knows you, it's your responsibility to know him. You can come sit up in here, or up in any sanctuary and claim to know God. You can also claim to come here to hear his word being prophesied! But if you walk up in here, and you don't feel his spirit, you're in the wrong place! Can you feel the holy spirit? Can you hear the spirit of the living God up in this church as only you can? Father, you know exactly who walked through these doors with a heavy heart, unsure and yearning for understanding. No matter how minute it may seem, you called them holy. You made them worthy of partnership. They are envied by many, dear God, because you invited them to a table that only some can stare at."

Service was fantastic! We genuinely enjoyed the love, the message, and the spirit of the Lord we felt up in the church home. I can't wait to go back. I never in my life thought that those words would ever linger from my tongue. I swore that I would never attend another church. I am glad that we gave this small intimate church an opportunity.

On our way home, we stopped by Wasabi's for dinner. We had a great discussion about church service, and we all promised to attend again soon. Angel became cranky, and I still had a few things to do before school tomorrow, so I was past ready to leave. After several attempts at comforting her and trying to soothe her, Charmaine and Calvin began getting fidgety and obviously ready to go as well. I glanced over at Marco, and he was shaking like a leaf. "Well, everyone, it's time to wrap it up. Some little person needs a nap?" Calvin said as he waved the waiter over to bring the bill.

Out of the corner of my eye, I felt someone staring in the distance. I didn't want it to appear obvious, but I had to look to make sure that I wasn't losing it. Sure enough, it was the Assistant Bishop Larry Brown, Marco's biological father. He was leaned up against a far wall watching us. I assumed he had given up messing with us, but it is obvious he hasn't.

I lightly kicked Charmaine under the table and guided her eyes to him. He stood looking down on us as though he had no fear of being seen. He had a cocky demeanor. Neither of us said anything to the guys, we just continued gathering our items and preparing to leave. I noticed when we stood to leave, he left out first. Calvin left as well to pull the car around. We loaded up and pulled off heading home.

We arrived home within no time. I confirmed the drop off time for Angel in the morning with Charmaine. I was excited to attend a new school and meet other people. We thanked Calvin and Charmaine for a beautiful day as we exited their car. It felt good to finally be at home. I bathed Angel, changed, and fed her, and readied myself for a good night's sleep. Marco pulled me in closer to him as we both drifted off to sleep. I was awakened at two a.m. by a noise outside of our window. It was hard for me to go back to sleep, and worry was not an emotion I wanted to visit. So, I began praying:

Your love and faithfulness, along with your goodness and mercy surround me daily Father. I will not fear whatever might come against me. My trust is in you God. I give thanks to you for your love and protection Father. In your son Jesus Christ's name, Amen.

The morning was here before we knew it. After my prayer, I dozed off and slept peacefully. I got up and readied myself before Marco so that I could wake Angel and get her dressed and fed. After I got Angel together, I put her in her swing in order to free myself to make Marco and I a couple of breakfast sandwiches. Marco entered the living area right on que. We loaded up the car and headed over to Charmaine's to drop off Angel, we then headed off to school. My stomach was in knots. I was excited and nervous. I glanced over at Marco, and he wore a blank nonchalant look.

"Well, I guess this is it," I said out loud to Marco. He never responded. He just parked and got out of the car like we were total strangers. His non-response almost pissed me off. I had to think about why he was reacting this way and decided that it wasn't worth me absorbing his negative energy. I am still going to make him a doctor's appointment though. His moods are becoming alarming.

"I need a copy of my schedule. I forgot to download it," I began. "Do you have yours?" I asked Marco as we walked up to the entrance in silence. He never responded. Now I'm pissed. I hadn't done anything to him, and I am tired of begging him to open up and talk to me. Once I realized that he wasn't speaking, I walked off and went about my business.

The office was packed with kids. I stood in line to await my turn. There was a guy standing in front of me that appeared as though he was an athlete. He was cute and appeared very well mannered. I listened to his conversation with the other students who walked up and greeted him. A young lady who may have been his girlfriend appeared out of nowhere and stood next to him in line. They made small conversation as they moved up. She must have said something funny to him because he broke out in a hearty laugh and looked around. When he looked back at me, our eyes locked until I broke the stare and looked away. "NEXT!" the office aide yelled. They both walked up to her desk together to handle whatever it was that they were here for. Within seconds, I was called up by a student aide who printed out my schedule. I left and proceeded to my first class of the day.

Before I realized it, it was lunch time. I grabbed an apple and decided to have lunch outside under a tree. Thank God I had lunch when I did, because my phone rang as soon as I took a seat on the ground. "Hello, may I speak with Ms. Ricks please?" the lady asked.

"This is her," I responded.

"Mrs. Ricks, this is Mrs. Johnson calling from Children's Service regarding Jermaine Johnson. We would like to set up an appointment to visit your residency. Would Thursday around four thirty be a suitable time?" she asked.

"Yes, it would. I will see you then," I stated before hanging up. Maybe I should have said no and scheduled it out for another week or so. Marco's behavior has become alarming.

Just as I got up off of the ground and brushed myself off, I saw the Assistant Bishop standing in the parking lot watching me. It made me feel uneasy, so I tried playing it off and rushed back into the school just as the return bell rang. I saw Marco hanging out at a young ladies locker smiling and laughing. I walked in his direction, and he ignored me.

Although my feelings were hurt, I kept on moving. I refuse to allow what he is going through to affect my own issues and desires. As I walked to my next class, I thought about my journey and my destiny. I am intentional about moving into my destiny. I am not about to sit around and wonder where I will be planted. If Marco wants to move on, he can. I cannot be fixated on him because God's plans for my life are bigger than he or I.

As I walked into class and took a seat, the guy from the office took a seat behind me. He tapped my shoulder and said, "Hello my name is

Joshua St. Clair, and you are?" I wasn't sure whether to respond or not. I wasn't trying to upset his lady friend as she walked into our same class.

I quickly said, "Kenna Ricks," and turned back around in time to catch her rolling her eyes at me. "I rebuke you Satan! You will have no power over my day," I said to myself.

I enjoyed class, it was Afrocentric Studies. It seems like it will be interesting. The rest of the day flew past. Eventually the bell rang for the last class of the day. My class was Home Economics. "Well, this should be fun," I thought until I saw Marco, the girl he was flirting with earlier and Joshua all in this class with me. Marco continued ignoring me, and I did him the same favor. Joshua on the other hand moved his chair next to me and wouldn't stop trying to make small talk. Class was fun and seemed as though it would be exciting. Once the bell rang, I went to my locker to get my items, and headed out to the car. Marco was nowhere in sight. I had to call Charmaine to get a ride home and boy was I pissed! "This will not happen to me again," I said out loud. I paced the sidewalk waiting for Charmaine to pick me up, and there he was again, the Assistant Bishop. Seeing that I was already in a mood, I marched over to him. "Can I help you with something, because now you are stalking me?" I said. He looked at me and laughed.

"Don't be foolish," he began. "I am waiting for my son," he said.

"Well, your son has left the building! I will tell him you are looking for him," I began saying before he cut me off.

"He knows I am here. Oh, he hasn't told you...?" he asked while laughing a hearty laugh and walking away.

"Told me what?" I asked. He jumped in his car and pulled away just as Charmaine pulled up.

Chapter Twenty-Six

Not Today Satan

O

nce I jumped in the car with Charmaine, I just broke down and started crying. I cried a good hearty cry because I was tired. I was tired of going through things, I was tired of fighting, I was tired of being mistreated, and I was tired of trusting people that turned on me as soon as my guard was down. I just want to take Angel and run! Charmaine pulled over in order to try and console me. She did the best that she knew how. She had no idea why I was so upset, nor what to say.

Eventually, Charmaine pulled off the side of the road, and found a park. A park seemed to be a better option. She parked the car and turned to me. With pleading eyes, she asked," What's wrong?" I tried explaining how my entire day went. I filled her in on what happened during the middle of the night, and how I had to pray. She sat calmly and listened without saying a word during my rant. When I stopped talking and crying, Charmaine began, "You've been through a lot, how can I help you to feel better?" she asked. I sat for a minute. I wanted to make sure that my next moves would be beneficial to my healing and growth and not just an emotional choice. I needed to be free of Marco in order to gain my independence.

"Can you please take me to the License Bureau to get my temporary drivers package? I need to take my test and pay for driving classes. I feel like in order to care for Angel and handle my other business, schooling, and whatever else, I need a vehicle."

Charmaine rubbed my arm and said, "Definitely honey! We can go take care of some of that stuff now," she responded.

Charmaine pulled off and headed to the nearest Department of Motor Vehicles and allowed me to go in and get a temporary package. I came back out and googled a driving school and paid my fees. Charmaine then took me to a car dealership and allowed me to purchase a car and put it in her name until I took my driving test. I found a twenty twenty-one Kia Optima. I wrote a check for my purchase; she signed the papers and we left. Calvin would have to come back with her tomorrow to pick the car up.

"Thank you for everything Charmaine," I began. "The last thing on my list is to find another home. Marco can have the one we are in, I don't care," I said.

"We can go online and look at some homes," Charmaine began.

"That sounds great!"

"Keep me posted on your choices so that we can make appointments to do walk-throughs," she responded. It was getting late, and Angel was hungry and restless. Charmaine dropped us off at home and promised that she and Calvin would take me to get my car after school and help me look for a new home.

Tomorrow, I will reschedule the visit with children's service as well. I am not situated enough to take on two more people at this time. Angel was enough for right now. I walked into the house to Marco laying on the couch watching television. I kept going. I didn't say a word. I took Angel to the back and sat her down while I made her a bottle. I went back into the room, stripped her down, bathed her, and put her to bed. I went into the kitchen and fixed myself a peanut butter and jelly sandwich and took it to the back with a nice cold glass of milk. I showered, pulled my clothes out for school, fixed Angels bag, and finally laid down and took my bible out.

I am pissed off! I have done everything that God wanted me to do but continue to go through hell!

God, I am overwhelmed. I feel like I am the only one who understands what I am up against. I am human, and I know I am just lost in my feelings at the moment. I don't want to feel as though I have to constantly defend myself. I don't want anything stolen from me, be it my happiness, my peace, or my piece of mind. I want to continue to experience transformation so that my elevation will look like an exaggeration of your word. I want my choices to be spirit-led. I feel the devil riding my back, yet I am faithful. Father allow me to touch glory through my actions. I promise I'm trying to hold on to my burdens and carry the cross, although I feel emotionally drained.

Father, help me to stay close to the power that has resurrected me, this way nothing anyone says or does can touch me. You have shown me on many occasions that my transformation may require me to walk this walk alone, and I am trying to be fine with not having company. I just need to know that it's your will and not my way that dictates the outcome. Father continue to place me in front of my blessing. I want to make things happen, even though it shouldn't be possible. I want to run full speed ahead toward my opportunities. I want to make you proud through my actions. I want to be spirit led. Place me in front of my blessings and lead me toward the blueprints of success. Amen.

I awoke feeling rejuvenated. I got up and entered Angel's room and she was gone. Marco was gone as well. I called Charmaine and asked if she had spoken to Marco. I was light weight hoping that he had dropped Angel off to her, although it sounded farfetched. I didn't want to panic. "No, I haven't," she began responding. "Let me ask Calvin, he's preparing for work." I waited patiently on the phone for Charmaine to ask Calvin had he spoken to Marco and briefed him on what was going on. Calvin said no, but didn't feel good about none of this, especially since Larry Brown the Assistant Bishop was in town.

"I know that you are worried and afraid," Calvin began. "Go on to school and let me find Marco and Angel," he said. I didn't agree with him, but I had to. I was not okay with going to school knowing that my baby was missing. How was I supposed to concentrate?

Charmaine jumped in and said, "Kenna please get ready for school. I will help Calvin locate Angel and Marco and return her safely to you. Babe, I will be by to pick you up and drop you off. Please give me forty-five minutes honey. We love you!" she stated.

I hung up to prepare myself for my day. I decided to call Mr. Singfield to see if he'd heard from Marco. Mr. Singfield informed me that he hadn't seen or heard from Marco. I was shocked and somewhat surprised. I filled Mr. Singfield and Agnes in as best I could on what was going on and what my intentions were. They felt horrible for me and told me if I needed them, not to hesitate to call. I thanked them both and sat on my couch awaiting Charmaine. I will go to school, but I am not staying. Sorry Charmaine and Calvin but Marco took it too far!

I had everything I needed and was ready when Charmaine showed up. When she beeped her horn, I went out and prepared to hear her speech. Everything went in one ear and out the other. I didn't want to upset her in any way. Her and Calvin were all that I had. I felt like leaving the security of my baby up to anyone else, was not being responsible.

We arrived at my school and Marco's car was nowhere in sight. I was beginning to get angrier and angrier. "Charmaine, I am sorry, but I cannot and will not promise that I will be in school all day," I began. "I can't concentrate knowing that Angel may not be safe. Especially with the way Marco has been lately," I said.

"I understand Kenna, just call me if you want to leave and I will come pick you up, or I'll send Calvin. Please honey, don't just leave. Calvin and I got you," she said.

I responded, "Okay," but it wasn't okay because I meant exactly what I said.

The bell rang to go to my first block class. I couldn't concentrate on anything in the world. My mind was all over the place. "Are you okay?" Joshua asked.

"Yes, I am fine, thanks," I responded.

"Well, you aren't your normal bubbly self. You aren't smiling and I don't feel that good vibe that radiates off of you. I'm not trying to irritate you or anything, but that is what attracted me to you," he explained as he sat next to me and continued staring.

"You should be walking in confidence, my child. You are beyond this world. Heaven is providing heavenly security. Walk in confidence my child, you have been blessed to walk in captivity by your blessings. Rebuke the darkness of your world and use it as your backdrop. This will allow you to bury your stress in the ashes of your worry."

"Thank you father," I said out loud, not realizing that Joshua was still staring me down. I felt a little better knowing that God was still walking this out with me and in control. I turned and looked at Joshua with the smile he spoke of and said, "Thank you, I needed you to snap me out of that."

"There's that smile," he responded back as we both turned to continue listening to Ms. Watson explain our lesson for today.

The bell rang, and there was still no call from Charmaine or Calvin. Marco wasn't anywhere to be found either. I proceeded to my next class and began to feel dizzy; I am sure it is because I was worrying and hadn't eaten. I tried not to, but as a mother it's just instinct. I laid my head down on my desk hoping that the feeling would go away. The strangest thing in the world happened to me. I saw Angel. It was like I was having some type of vision. Larry Brown was around her. But why, why is...Oh my God! I need to get out of here!

I ran out of class and out of the school. Joshua was hot on my heels. "Hey Kenna, where are you going?" he asked.

"Joshua!" I screamed and cried. "PLEASE, I have to go! Someone has kidnapped my daughter and I need to rescue her. I can't do this right now!" I said as I continued running toward the main street and away from the school.

"Kenna, I can take you! Hold up!" he yelled. I was out of breath and out of answers. I know what I see, and I know what God has said. I am lost as to what I am supposed to do with it all. I guess I could let Joshua give me a ride. The Uber I planned to call may take a while.

Joshua pulled up and I jumped in his car. I wasn't crying as hard because my head began to hurt. "Look Kenna, I don't know you, I just know what I feel. Can I ask you a question or two?" he asked.

"Yes sure," I responded.

"First of all, where do you need to go? Secondly, do you have any idea who has your daughter? Could it be her father or someone he knows?" Joshua asked innocently although it still made my blood boil.

"Can you give me one second Joshua? I will answer you. I need to make a call first," I said. I pray that she picks up.

Chapter Twenty-Seven

God See's All Things

"Hello Charmaine," I began.

"Hello Kenna, can I call you right back?" she said before I could get out another word.

"I'd prefer you meet me at the car dealership in ten minutes," I was able to say before the line clicked over. "Joshua, if you don't mind, could you run me by the Kia dealership off of Arlington. I will explain as much as I can while we wait for her," I said. "Joshua, I don't know why I am about to spill my guts to you, but I need to tell someone outside of God. It has gotten to a point where the people I trusted when I moved here are being exposed as not being trustworthy. I grew up in an abusive home. Both of my parents were involved in a Mega church that could be considered more like a cult. I, along with others, were made to do ungodly things with our Bishop, Assistant Bishop, and other church members. If I didn't do those things, my parents as well as other church heads would discipline me and the others severely.

We were being taught scripture in a way in which it justified their wrong doings. I had no outside friends except Marco. Marco and his family attended the church as well. Marco was quiet and somewhat withdrawn during those times. He went through his own stresses at school and being bullied. This is actually how we began our friendship. He may not have spoken much, but he was very observant and began noticing my behavior and bruises.

I began confiding in him, and he in me. I was fed up and mustered up the courage to take the entire operation down with the help of Marco. But not before the Bishop beat me to a point of almost losing my life. My parents were arrested and charged with child endangerment and abuse. They were released and the entire case and situation disappeared because of the connections the Bishop had. They were re-arrested on additional charges after we had the church raided. What didn't disappear was the fact that the Bishop had gotten me pregnant. I mustered up enough courage along with Marco to shut their entire operation down because we were able to provide evidence.

To sum everything up because there are too many details and too long of a story. Marco's mother was the church secretary. Unbeknown to Marco's father, Mr. Singfield, Marco's mother was the one setting everything up along with the Bishop and his First Lady. But get this, Marco's dad Mr. Singfield, we later found out wasn't even his biological father. His father is the Assistant Bishop Larry Brown. One of the people who raped and abused me. The Bishop is my daughter's father. He is in jail, along with his wife, Marco's mom, and several other church members," I began telling Joshua. He listened intently without interrupting and seemed genuinely concerned.

I didn't want to overwhelm Joshua, but I wanted someone to know what was going on just in case I needed back up. Just as we pulled up, Charmaine and Calvin were pulling up. Joshua jumped out of the car with a smile on his face," Hey Uncle Calvin," he said smiling and walking over to greet Calvin with a hug. I was more shocked and dumbfounded than I was anything else. What in the world is going on here? I walked over to get answers for myself.

"Uncle Calvin, Joshua?" I asked.

Joshua laughed before saying," My father is the Captain at the Police Department. He and Uncle Calvin go back a long way. I was about four or five when I first met him," Joshua explained. I was able to breathe a sigh of relief after hearing his explanation. This was getting a little too weird for my liking. I noticed that Charmaine didn't join us. She has been acting just as weird as her brother lately. I don't know what those two are up to, but I'm going to play like I don't see what's going on.

I really need to speak to Calvin alone, but she doesn't let him out of her eyesight. While she sat in their car on the phone, I took the opportunity to ask Calvin a few questions. "Not to interrupt you fella's, but Calvin, no word on Angel or Marco?" I asked.

He looked slightly over to see if Charmaine was looking and then said, "No, but I am going to speak with the Captain and put a warrant out for his arrest for kidnapping. Charmaine disagrees with me and personally, I don't care. She has been acting very strange since she visited her mother," Calvin complained. My antenna went up. Charmaine hasn't divulged that information to me I thought. Calvin went on to say, "I thought it was a bad idea myself, but she wanted to make peace with her alone. So, I said whatever. She hasn't brought it back up, and nor have I asked about the visit. Hell, I thought it was a bad idea for Marco to meet with Larry after all that Mr. Singfield has done for him, but I guess my opinion doesn't matter much, so I keep it to myself," Calvin said just as Charmaine exited their car and walked in our direction. As disappointed as I was, I couldn't act on it until I was able to get my car.

Calvin ended up driving my car back to the house. I had him put it in the garage seeing that Marco never parks in there. I pray Charmain doesn't tell him I purchased it. I rode home with Joshua and continued filling him in on Charmaine and Calvin. I explained how I had no idea Charmaine visited her and Marco's mom at the jail. Nor did I know that Marco had met up with his biological father. The last conversation Charmaine and I had about that was her saying that she was waiting for Calvin to get approval for all of us to go. We planned to go and sincerely forgive them all and make that the last time we even dealt with this mess.

"Wow," Joshua began. "This is definitely a lot. If there is one thing that I know about Uncle Calvin, is that he is fair and trustworthy. Charmaine must be really pissing him off," he said in a matter-of-fact way.

We arrived at the house a little before Calvin, and Marco still wasn't there. That was a good sign. Calvin pulled my car into the garage and soon Charmaine arrived to pick him up. I waved at them both and said thank you! "No problem Kenna," Calvin began. "I will give you a call tomorrow," Calvin said as he got in the car with Charmaine. I thanked Joshua and apologized for bogging him down with all of my issues.

"Kenna, you aren't bogging me down. I asked and volunteered. Believe it or not, I saw you in church Sunday and was mesmerized by you. When I saw you in school, I said God sure answered my prayers." I looked at him a little confused, what did he mean answered his prayers? There is no better way of knowing the truth than to ask, I thought.

"Joshua, what about the girl that I have been seeing you around school with, I thought that she was your girlfriend?" I asked.

Joshua shook his head before saying, "Everyone thinks that she is my girl. No, that is my sister who just happens to be a self-assertive brat. She is very touchy and feely with me. People who don't know us assume the very thing you have. She has been like that with me since I was a baby. She can be overbearing and overprotective."

"Oh okay," I laughingly said to Joshua as I was prepared to exit his car. Well, what do you know, I thought to myself. I was just about to exit the car and Marco pulled up in the driveway and exited carrying Angel into the house. He never even looked this way. I was fuming! I caught an instant attitude. Let me call Calvin to let him know that Marco has shown up and ask him, what should I do? I think it would be best if I packed her and I a bag and headed to a hotel. I will catch an Uber to school If I have to. "Give me one second Joshua. I need to pack a bag, and if you don't mind could you drop us off at the nearest hotel please?"

"Sure," Joshua responded. "I am here for whatever you need," he said.

Once I exited the car and entered the house, Marco had Angel in her swing. She was fast asleep as he sat and shook like crazy. I walked around him and grabbed my baby to take her to the back room. "You know I wouldn't hurt Angel or put her in harm's way," he said in a matter- of- fact way. "I just wanted to spend some time with her alone. I wanted to see how it felt to love a child with your entire heart that was not your actual seed," Marco began saying. "I saw Larry Brown. He explained to me what happened between him and my mother, and why she hid him from me. He was married and his wife had no idea that my mother and he were sneaking around. He claimed he never stopped loving me or Mark. He gave her money and would keep up with us through her. He asked for my forgiveness, and I gave it to him, Kenna," he continued. "We spoke about Mr. Singfield and how great of a father and role model he was to me and my brother. He also spoke about how hard it probably was for Mr. Singfield after he found out that he wasn't our biological father.

"Marco, I don't want to hear anything that monster of a donor has said to you! You may have forgiven him, but it doesn't mean that I have to because you have. When I am ready, if I am ever ready, I will do it from my heart, not yours! His admission of guilt does not excuse the fact that he raped and molested me! I was a child! Nor does it give you the right to kidnap my child without my knowledge, you have truly crossed the line this time!"

"Listen Marco, you know better than anyone what I have suffered. It is justifiable for me to be selfish and protective of myself and my child. What I will not tolerate is being taken for granted, taken advantage of, and being lied to. I can no longer stay here with you! Angel and I are out of here! You can have this house and that messy life of lies and betrayal. I don't owe anyone anything," I said as I packed up as much of mine and Angels stuff as I could.

I took Angel out to the car first. Joshua got out of the car to assist me. I headed back into the house to retrieve more of our items and noticed Marco heading out the door with a hammer and screaming obscenities. I screamed for Joshua to look out, but it was too late. I quickly dialed 911, and then Calvin and filled him in. I rushed over and tried helping Joshua. He outpowered Marco and managed to restrain him up against the car. Blood was all over Joshua, and I felt horrible for even involving him. Marco had lost his mind! I just thank God his aim was off! Although there appeared to be a lot of blood, Joshua had a deep gash over his eyebrow that could have been worse than it appeared to be. He would definitely need a few stitches.

Calvin pulled up at the same time as the other units and Joshua's father. He was understandably heated and had no understanding of what was going on. An ambulance was called for Joshua, and Marco was hauled off to jail. Charmaine never called to check on me or anything. What's so crazy is the fact that her non-action spoke volumes. God knows all things, spoken and unspoken.

Chapter Twenty-Eight

Weirder Things Have Happened
One Year Later

A
lot has happened in a year's time. I got my license and bought my own home. I graduated, finishing out the year home schooled. I have two classes remaining to complete before I am given custody of Candies son and my brother. Our visits and transformation has been going great. My hearing for both is approaching and I am extremely excited.

After appearing at Marco's hearings and watching how weird Charmaine had begun acting, I cut her off as well. Calvin left her after the fiasco with Joshua and Marco.

Joshua and I have been dating and going to church on a regular basis. I enjoy their church and plan to make it my church home soon. Although I have been faithful to attending, I have not committed fully as a member.

Joshua's family along with Calvin and Mr. Singfield have truly been my support system, and Ms. Agnes keeps me together. Marco from what I heard received five years in a Mental Rehabilitation Center. Charmaine may need to be in there with him. Maybe whatever the both of them are experiencing mentally is hereditary.

Calvin was telling us that she doesn't even practice law anymore. She has no real income and lives in a subsidized housing unit. That blew my mind. Larry Brown is still in town, somewhere. Calvin had him under surveillance, until Larry Brown began complaining to the Police Department that he was being harassed. He was last spotted coming out of a Residence Inn on the Northside of town.

I decided to get a job so that my money would last a while longer. I was hired as a receptionist at the church four days a week. Agnes and Mr. Singfield enjoyed watching Angel for me, and the days they couldn't Calvin did.

Everything was going good until one day, while at work, I was served paperwork from the courts regarding Mr. Charles Jackson and paternity. The Bishop wanted a DNA test performed on Angel. I don't care what he wants! If I have to, I will submit, but not if I have other options. He will never see her, so I don't get why he wants to go through all of this.

I called the courts to inquire about my rights and to request a court appointed attorney. I am a victim of rape, and the victimizer should not have any type of rights. Especially since I am not asking him to be responsible legally with support. I want him to leave me and baby Angel alone. Act as though we are nonexistent. I was given another phone number to call to inquire about legal aid and representation. I was also told by the courts that I had thirty days to comply. If I don't, I could be found in violation of a court order.

I rebuke you Satan in the name of the Father, the son, and the holy spirit! "Thank you for answering all of my questions and thank you for the information. I can take it from here," I said.

"God, I know the pats on my back that you are giving me, are given with love. I will burp out the desires that I know will put my stress to sleep. I am blessed and I am your child. I am the body that can't be bodied, destroyed, or tampered with. This is your fight! I trust and believe you have me protected."

I just sat at my desk and looked around. I began to relax. Just then, I heard my Father God speak:

I deserve your trust. I have not betrayed you. I care for you when no one else will. Take your lessons my child with a meek full heart. I give you red flags so that you don't have to deal with the blues. The belly of the beast cannot digest your anointing. Allow your spirit to lead you to your paradise of peace.

Thank you Father, thank you Lord, thank you! I have nothing left to lose. I am grateful for the gift of God to be on me. Nothing that I've endured has gone unrecognized by my Father God. Chains will be broken in this season, so I need to snap out of what I see with my physical eye's and continue using my spiritual vision. All things will work out for the good. "Have your way in my life Father, in every area. I pray this in your name Father God, Amen."

I finished my day at work, got Angel, and decided to have a relaxing evening alone at home. Although I began attending church again, it was important for me to study and do my own research. Whatever I need clear understanding in, I asked God for discernment to understand. My life's journey has taught me that a relationship with God has no boundaries or walls. A church home was supposed to be a place where worshiping our father took place. Nowadays, a lot of churches have gotten away from the spiritual meaning and have politicized and corrupted the church. They are filled with lying spirits, glamorizing the gospel. The gospel is a sacrifice not to be glamorized. God breathes over people that are in poverty and are in need. God will change their glory into shame.

My true church home is within me. Not with a den of thieves. Godless corruption can exist in a living room as well as during bible study in a church. The perception of Christianity has been hijacked. Until recently, I'd rather study, like I continue to do, and receive clarity through my Father God. I have the same number to the mainline as anyone else.

After I fed Angel and bathed her, I put her in bed for the night. I read and studied my scripture for the next hour and a half before getting up and preparing myself for bed. Just as I prepared to jump into the bed, I heard a knock on the door. Why wouldn't Joshua call me before he came by, I thought. Once I arrived at the door, I saw it was Charmaine. I just stared at her, not knowing what she wanted nor what

I was supposed to say. My first thought was, how did she know where I was staying?

"I followed you from the church," she said before I could ask the question. "I am sorry Kenna; I am so sorry! I don't know what got into me. This feels like a nightmare, where I just awoke to nothing and no answers. I can't begin to explain what happened. One minute, I went to the jail to offer forgiveness so that I could move forward with a cleansed heart, and the next minute, I felt possessed. Please don't turn your back on me, I need you Kenna!" Charmaine practically begged.

I allowed her to have a seat. I also offered Charmaine a cup of coffee or tea. She said no to either but did ask for water. I gave her bottled water and sat down across from her open to hear what she had to say. While she spoke, I prayed for her spirit. "Kenna, you know me, and you know that I wouldn't intentionally deceive you," she began.

"But you did," I responded before she could finish. "Look Charmaine, if you are looking for forgiveness or asking for forgiveness, I forgive you. What I can't ever do again is allow you to bring your negative spirit back into my life. I choose to love you from a distance. You and Marco both came for me at the same time. You both knew that I had no one outside of either of you. I guess that held no importance to either of you, but it was a red flag for me. Right now, I am focused on me and Angel and not the past," I said with a little hostility in my voice.

Charmaine looked up at me like she was morphing into something or someone outside of herself. She just stared at me for a minute before I interrupted whatever thought she may have had. "It was good seeing you, but I need to lay down," I stated. Her entire demeanor changed just that rapidly. She went from being a sympathetic friend to looking like something out of a scary movie. I stood up as a sign for her to follow suit and exit my home. She took her time, but eventually stood. I walked behind her to the door because I wanted to make sure that she made it to the door and nowhere else. If she would have tried anything,

I'd be repenting right now because she would have gotten just what her and her devil came for. Before she walked out, she looked back at me and smiled. I closed and locked the door quickly. I made sure that all of the windows and doors were secured before I went back to my room and laid down.

I had a missed call on my phone from Joshua, I hurried to call him back. "Hey babes, how was your day?" he asked.

"It was okay, outside of being served a summons for DNA and Charmaine popping up at my house acting possessed," I said with a smidge of laughter.

"Whoa, wait a minute! What did you say?" he asked.

"You heard me Joshua," I responded.

"That's wild! If the Bishop is never getting out, what difference does it make whose child Angel is?" he asked. "As for Charmaine, I wouldn't let her anywhere near the inside of my house after how she played you and Uncle Calvin," he said, sounding a little pissed off.

"You are right babe. I only answered the door because I thought it was you. Once I opened it and saw that it wasn't, she began apologizing. I told her that I forgave her, but I no longer wanted to be bothered. That's about when she began her transformation. Her eyes became dark and hollow, it was like something out of a scary movie. I politely told her that it was time for her to leave," I continued explaining.

"Kenna, if you don't mind," Joshua began. "I think it would be best if I came and stayed a few nights. I want to make sure that you and Angel are okay. I will be worried sick knowing that Charmaine has found you. There is no telling what she is up to," he explained.

"Joshua, talk to your parents first and see how they feel about you staying over. After being hit with that hammer by Marco, I've been a little leery of inviting you over, especially overnight," I said.

"I will do just that Kenna. Give me a few minutes to discuss this with them, and I will give you a call back."

Just When You Thought All Had Failed

I

was tired emotionally more than anything. I ended up falling asleep awaiting Joshua's call back. I began to awaken once I heard Angel crying. I was a little unsure of how long I had been asleep, but it must have been long enough for her to need her diaper changed and possibly a nice warm bottle. I turned over and noticed that Calvin and Joshua both called me about ten times. It must be urgent, I thought. Let me call Calvin back, and then I will call Joshua. "Hello Calvin, what's going on?" I began asking. "I just woke up from a nap and saw that you called me several times."

"Kenna, I just pulled in your driveway along with several other officers," Calvin began. "What? What's going on Calvin?" I asked as I approached the door to allow Calvin in to explain. "A neighbor called the station and reported suspicious activity going on out in front of this address," Calvin explained as he and a few officers moved in and began searching the premises.

"What suspicious activity are they talking about?!" I demanded to know. "Calvin, please tell me what activity!" I screamed out now panicking. Joshua and his father showed up. He held me as I cried out of fear of the unknown. "Oh shoot, I almost forgot to check on Angel!" I said as I jerked loose from Joshua; he was heavy on my heels. I went to check on Angel. She was gone, nowhere to be found.

I screamed and cried to the top of my lungs. Father, why! Please, show me mercy! I just can't take it anymore. I am human! Calvin walked back into the room and took a seat across from where Joshua and I were.

"Kenna, I just received a call this afternoon that the Bishop, his wife, your mother as well as Charmaine and Marco's mother, have been released and are on probation. Your father is still in prison from what we know. I'm not sure which judge allowed this nonsense, but it's true. We believe that...,"

"Detective, could you come here for a second sir?" one of the officers asked Calvin.

"One sec," Calvin responded to me before getting up to see what the officer wanted.

"Detective, this screen is sliced, and the latch has been broken. This had to be the access point. We are dusting for prints and there are footprints leading around the back of the house," the officer reported.

"Get the impressions of the footprints and see if there are any tire tracks. Also, talk to the neighbors. Go door to door and ask questions, anything that you can think to do. Make sure to canvass the block to see if any neighbors have cameras. If so, check the camera around the approximate time for anything or people acting suspicious heading in this direction. Go to the neighbor's house who reported the suspicious activity, and let's see what they have! I want this case treated with care and urgency!" Calvin ordered.

"Yes sir, detective." Joshua's father was already on it. He'd left out in search of cameras, door cameras, or any evidence that may lead back to who we already knew was behind this mess.

"We have them on camera." Joshua's father re-entered several minutes later, announcing to Calvin. "An elderly neighbor said that she was the one who called in the suspicious activity. She's been keeping an eye out over here especially since she noticed a lady lingering around out front in the evenings. The lady's suspicious behavior had her taking pictures of her getting in and out of her car. She also witnessed her walking around doing nothing. The neighbor gave me these pictures. I was not shocked to see that it was Charmaine."

"She went on to say that she made the call because a couple of hours ago, that same lady came back with three other people. A gentleman got out of the car with her, and they walked around the back. She noticed that they came back around hurriedly with what looked like something wrapped up in a blanket. The only reason she knew that there were two other people was because they started arguing outside of the car for whatever reason. The neighbor took pictures of everything, even their license plate."

Calvin showed me and Joshua the pictures. Sure, enough it was the Bishop, Charmaine, the First lady, and Charmaine and Marco's mom. I looked on in shock, and then looked up at Calvin. "What's wrong Kenna," he asked.

"I was expecting to see my mother with them, and she's not."

"Your mother from my understanding was released along with the others but hasn't been seen with them.

Joshua's father called the station immediately, "This is Captain St. Clair, I want an amber alert to be put out for baby Angel Ricks. She is a one-year-old female African American baby. She was kidnapped from her home about two hours ago. She was last seen being carried away by these four suspects, Charmaine Campbell- Body, Charles Jackson, Angela Brown-Jackson, and Caroline Campbell-Singfield. I want a warrant issued, and all available cars on the lookout for a 2012 grey Kia Sophia with a license plate of Alpha Beta Car 9067. They should be considered armed and dangerous. I will send over all the recent photos as soon as we hang up."

"Got it Captain, and I am on it."

"I will have this house under heavy surveillance, Kenna. We will find baby Angel. Let's pray, so that we can get to work," Mr. St. Clair said. We stood and grabbed hands:

Father, Simply speak. I need you to allow us to see past these painful moments, and still be able to produce seed. A seed that holds enough power to bruise the head of the serpent. Father, we know that you will give someone a promise in the most painful time of their life. If we can see past what's in the moment, the pain and disappointment will only cause Kenna to limp, but she will still be able to keep moving. You have the final say, allow her to continue to produce in your name Father, Amen.

I felt a load lifted off of me at that very moment. More than two were gathered in the holy Father's name, touching, and agreeing.

"Dad, would it be okay if I stayed to keep Kenna company?" Joshua asked his father.

"Sure son, you know how to call if an emergency arises. You both stay safe and check in."

"Thanks dad, I will be home early in the morning before school to change and prepare. I just wouldn't feel right leaving her here alone."

"It's fine son."

"Love you dad, and Uncle Calvin."

We all hugged it out before everyone left from the inside of my home. Police were outside parked on the street in undercover cars all night.

Joshua called and came over the next few days and stayed with me. I was so thankful and grateful for him. We lay snuggled up on the couch watching television when a breaking story interrupted the program.

BREAKING NEWS: "There was a massive shooting at a Holiday Inn Hotel in Copley Township. Four individuals who were wanted and considered armed and dangerous have all been pronounced dead on scene. Baby Angel Ricks is safe and in the hands of Captain St. Clair and Detective Evans of the Mecklenburg County Police Department." I looked and was at a loss for words. "Mrs. Camilla Ricks, do you have anything to say for yourself?" the news reporters asked. As I looked on, I was in utter disbelief. I hadn't seen my mother in some time. She had truly aged beautifully. She turned to the camera's and said, "I didn't protect my daughter the first time these animals tried destroying her because I was a big part of the problem. I couldn't stand back and allow them to do it to my granddaughter, so I did what I had to do and called the police my damn self."

I cried. Mama! My mother looked strong and fearless. She had never appeared strong to me. "Call your dad or Calvin, Joshua! I need to know what is going on," I said in between good tears. My mother saved my Angel although she couldn't save me, her words I repeated out loud. I sat back on the couch thanking God for Angels safety as well as for my mother. I want to see her and thank her personally. I want to let her know that I forgive her.

"Hello son," the Captain answered his phone and said.

"Dad, we are watching everything on the news," Joshua responded.

"Yes son, I can't talk too much right now though. I have paperwork I have to do and others to interview. I will have one of my men come by and fill you two in or give you instructions on where to meet us with Angel. Love you son."

"I love you more dad," Joshua said before hanging up his line.

I gave Joshua the biggest hug ever. "Thank you for being here to help me Joshua. I owe you, your dad, and Calvin the world."

"You don't owe me anything. Your friendship and your smile is gratitude enough," Joshua began saying as he hugged me while looking into my eyes.

"Kenna, I don't know what it is about you outside of your obvious beauty that is drawing me in to you, but I really like you. I want to see you and Angel safe and happy."

"Thank you Joshua," I responded. I gave Joshua a peck on his lips before going into the kitchen to fix us both a couple of sandwiches.

Chapter Thirty

Turning Pages

A

ngel was returned to me after she was checked out by the paramedics. Calvin advised me to take her over to Children's Hospital if she begins acting differently or if I notice bruising or she begins crying for extended periods of time. No telling what any of them would do to her to get back at me. I made a call to Mr. Singfield and he and Agnes came right over. Calvin ended up coming by as well as both of Joshua's parents. I noticed that his sister never comes, nor does she speak to me.

We sat around talking and laughing. It felt good to just relax and enjoy one another's company without stress or worry. Calvin said that my mother would be given an attorney. He and the Captain will try and help her in any way possible. She did tell Calvin that she wants to see me, so I plan to see her in a couple of days. Calvin looked at me and shook his head before saying, "You know your mother is pleading not guilty. She claims that they tried killing her, and she wasn't ready to die twice."

Days became weeks, and weeks turned into months. Angel had her first birthday party and it turned out really nice. I was able to visit my mom and truly forgive her. We talk on the phone every day and Angel and I visit her often. After the funerals of the others, we all promised to keep the memory of each of them dead.

The boys were permanently in my custody. It was a slight adjustment, but with Mr. Singfield and Ms. Agnes, Calvin, and Joshua they stayed busy. Calvin and Marco encouraged me to go to college online. I thought that it would be a wonderful idea, so I enrolled in Yale University's Theology degree program. I seem to be doing an excellent job. I also decided to do my internship in Rome. Calvin volunteered to keep the boys and Ms. Agnes and Mr. Singfield welcomed Angel to stay with them when the time came for me to leave. Although I do not want to depart from the kids. Yet, I know I am being prepared for a higher calling in my life.

Four Years Later

Time has definitely flown by. Angel will be five years old soon. I have one year left until I graduate college. I plan to leave for Rome in two weeks. I have prepared, saved, and made sure that the kids will be taken care of. I will be away for approximately a year. Joshua and I are still dating. He plans to bring the kids to see me for my birthday. That will be so exciting. He will also stay at my house while I am away and help out with the kids, giving the others a much-needed break.

We were leaving counseling at the church and stopped by the store to pick up a few last-minute items for dinner. I noticed that Joshua continued looking out of his rearview mirror, but I didn't know why. Once we pulled into the parking lot, he just sat for a minute as though he was trying to get his nerves together.

"Are you okay Joshua?" I asked.

"Yes babe, I am fine," Joshua responded back. I thought nothing else about it as he exited the car to make our purchases and returned.

Once we arrived home, we put the kids to bed. It was time for me and Joshua to have some much-needed quality time. When Joshua and I first began dating, I expressed the fact to him that I wanted to remain celibate until marriage. I was traumatized behind all that I had gone through and was truly scared to allow myself to love in that way. Joshua had been so loving and patient with me. He hasn't forced me, nor has he been unfaithful.

Tonight, felt different. I wanted to make love to him. I prayed about it and asked for forgiveness ahead of time. I wanted him. We both took our time showering like normal. He had no idea that I wanted to make love to him. He lay in the bed waiting to snuggle up like we always do. I exited the bathroom in a beautiful negligee that I bought for this occasion. He watched as I entered the room and sat down on the bed next to him. I saw the sparkle in his eyes and watched as the biggest smile spread across his face.

"Are you sure?" he asked.

I shook my head, "Yes."

Joshua and I made love all night. We fell asleep and woke up several times throughout the night. We made love over and over until neither of us could move. This was the best night of my life. I felt so loved and wanted. Before either of us knew what time it was, the kids were up in the living area screaming and playing. I got up in order to fix their breakfast and quiet down the noise.

"Paul, Jermaine, and Miss Angel, have a seat right this second!" I began saying sternly. "You all are old enough to know better than to run through here with all that screaming and playing. Have a seat in front of that television until I am done cooking breakfast! Do you all hear and understand me?" I asked.

"Yes," all three answered back.

After I fixed their breakfast, I took Joshua his breakfast into the room. He thanked me and said that I didn't have to do it. In my head, I was thinking, you deserve that and more. I allowed him to eat in peace, returning to the kitchen in order to clean up and finish washing dishes. I had the boys gather the trash to take out back, and Angel helped wipe off the table. I sent them all to their rooms to make their beds and to tidy up. They took their showers and prepared to get dressed. When I returned to my room, Joshua was in the shower singing. I took his plate to the kitchen and washed it before I returned to get myself prepared for the day.

When Joshua exited the bathroom, he informed me that for the next several days, he may not see me much or at all. He has mandatory overtime and will be working twelve-to-fourteen-hour days. I didn't like it much, but I understood. Especially once he made it clear that he needed to make and save as much as possible. This way he would have no issues bringing the kids to visit. He leaned in and gave me a kiss before exiting out the door. I took my shower and thanked God continually for gifting me with such an honorable and loving young man.

The next several days went past fast. Although I missed Joshua here with us physically, we talked on the phone, and he Face Timed me from work several times a day. I was packed up and ready to go. Calvin came by and picked up the boys and Mr. Singfield and Agnes came and picked up Angel. Calvin and I Face Timed until my Uber arrived.

"Well, sounds like my ride has arrived, I will hit you up once I land," I informed Joshua.

"I love you, safe travels," Joshua said with tear-filled eyes.

"I love you more, Mr. St. Clair," I responded while allowing my tears to smother my face.

I grabbed my bags and my purse and headed out. I jumped in the backseat of the Uber and laid my head back to relax. I was beginning to over think this trip and doubt myself. I know better than to do this. God has allowed me to withstand pain that was supposed to crush me. My presence will be felt, and many will thirst for my attention now that God got it. I am not regular, I am God's particular treasure, and I thank him.

Just as I finished up my thoughts, I happened to open my eyes and noticed that the driver was not heading in the direction of the airport. "Excuse me sir, where are we going? This is not the way to the airport," I said calmly but with concern. When he looked through the rearview mirror and I saw those eyes, I knew that God was about to take over. This was not about to be my fight. I had to stay calm and not panic. I dialed Calvin's number and continued asking questions so that Calvin could hear what was going on.

"Aren't you glad to see me?" he asked. I wanted to play it smart and not allow the devil himself to draw me in.

"Actually, I am happy to see you, despite what has happened to me because of you. I forgive you daddy. When were you released from jail, and why are you kidnapping me?" I said because I wanted Calvin to hear his response.

"Baby girl, I got out shortly after the others. I kept it a secret because I wanted to surprise you. I hear your mother has grown some balls and killed the others," he said laughingly. "She won't have another opportunity to go up against me after tonight and that's for sure."

"Dad, why are you kidnapping me, how did you find me?"

"STOP ASKING ME QUESTIONS, haven't you learned not to question shit I say?!"

That pissed me off! "It is considered kidnapping when you take someone against their will. I am supposed to be headed to the airport and you have me on two twenty-six north by the Northfield exit. In the complete opposite direction of the airport. I needed to give a description of the car to Calvin as well, so I just started rambling off," Kidnapping somebody in this raggedy two thousand three Shadow! To make it so bad the car is red! You are pathetic!" I said. I knew that would do it. He was ready to exit off the freeway in order to try and harm me. "I know this area. This is where Larry Brown is staying. I heard his crybaby self was out here." Just as we pulled off of the freeway, we were stuck behind a couple of cars. I saw my opportunity. I grabbed and began choking the life out of him. He tried wiggling loose, but God strengthened me, and I was able to hold on. He took his foot off of the gas, and the car rammed into the car in front of us. The gentleman got out and came to the car door and opened it after he noticed the scuffle. I began screaming, "He kidnapped me and that the police are on the way!" The guy helped subdue him, which was a huge relief.

Sirens were blaring in the distance, as my dad continued trying to free himself. I knew I was wrong but couldn't help myself. I hauled off and socked him in his nose. Once he said, "Ouch," I hit him again. Before I knew it, I was throwing a barrage of punches at him for all the pain he caused me. Once the police arrived and secured the area, I was able to stop and breathe.

I called Calvin back to thank him for being a godsend. He laughed before saying, "From what I am hearing, your dad needed protection." Calvin quickly switched up and began telling me that there were police units raiding the hotel where Larry Brown was staying. Calvin quickly stated that he'd call me back. Just as I lifted my finger to end the call, I heard him say, "Don't forget to call the airport about your missed flight."

I am glad he said that because it slipped my mind just that fast. I hung up my line, and my phone began ringing again, "Dang, "I thought until I looked and saw that it was Joshua calling me on facetime.

"Hey babe, are you okay?" he asked.

"Yes, a little shaken up, but I am fine."

"Dang," he began saying. "I couldn't imagine going through all that you have. I don't understand any of this myself. I just know that you have endured quiet a lot." I walked back and forth on the side of the road waiting to be transported to the airport. I thought about what Joshua was saying as well as everything that I have been through these last few years. I have nothing but gratitude for God. I refuse to bow out. I have been through too many breakthroughs to believe that what I am going through is strong enough to break me. I realize that I started feeling drained when I took my eyes off of the word of God and began watering the blind, instead of the vision I am trying to see. I am finally at a place in my life where I can honestly say that I forgive those who have trespassed against me.

"Josh babe, you don't understand it because it wasn't meant for you to understand. At times, I didn't understand either. Up until recently, I still questioned God as to "why." Until one day my bubble was busted when God responded," why not."

Chapter Thirty-One

Life Changing

I was picked up and transported to the airport. After explaining what happened, and trying to change my flight, I was finally booked on another airline. I had to wait a couple of hours before departure, so I called and checked on Angel. Ms. Agnes and Mr. Singfield said they were having a wonderful time with her. I called Calvin to check up on the boys. Calvin had the boys at the park playing basketball. They seemed to be having an amazing time. I decided not to call Joshua back. I wanted to give him some space. He doesn't need to be worried about me all day every day, it's not healthy.

I walked around the airport to waste some time. I still had another hour to burn, so I decided to find a nice cozy seat and read. I heard about a book called "Seven Deadly Sins, The Testimony of an OG" by Author Tray Real and Author X'Zalyn. Joshua's mother said that it was a must read, so I thought now would be the perfect time to relax, focus and read it.

I became so engrossed in the read, that I almost missed the call for my flight. People were lining up to board. I boarded and prepared myself for a long relaxing flight. While trying to focus on finishing up my read, I felt myself fighting sleep. I had no idea that my mind and body was this exhausted. When I awoke, we were told to remain seated until we saw the release light. At that time, we will be given further instructions and ushered off of our flight.

I have never in my life seen such a beautiful place on earth. I arrived at my dorm and fell back on my bed. I wanted to take in the fresh environment and air. This place is amazing, I thought! I had to shake myself out of my stuck frame of mind in order to get up, unpack my items and walk the campus. I wanted to make sure that my registration and paperwork was complete, so I headed to the registration office. After leaving registration, I decided to take the tour bus through the Colosseum, as well as the Lazio region. I've learned so much and genuinely enjoyed the tour.

I arrived back at my dorm feeling well informed and amazing. I decided to call and check on the kids and make sure that everything was going well. I didn't check in after I arrived, so I thought it was time to call to let everyone know that I made it safely. I called Calvin first and spoke with him and the boys, everything was going great. I hung up with him and called to check on Angel. Mr. Singfield and Agnes said that Angel was doing well. I finished up with them and called Joshua. I called Joshua on FaceTime. I wanted to see him; I missed him already. Joshua was preparing to go hang out with a couple of his buddies. Why did I get a little jealous is beyond me, but I did. I tried to hide it, but I was no good at it and my disappointment was noticeable.

"Babe, what's wrong?" Joshua asked.

"Nothing Joshua, I am okay babe. I just wanted to see you, and let you know that I made it here safely. Call me tomorrow babe and enjoy your night out," I said before quickly hanging up my line. How am I going to make it all the way over here for a year if I am feeling like this overnight? I need to regroup and get it together.

Days turned into weeks; time was definitely flying by. I'm not sure if it were food or water, but I couldn't keep anything down. I felt lethargic and couldn't stay awake. Sleep has become my friend. My classes were great and highly informative. If only I could stay awake through them all, I'd be good. It had gotten so bad that I made an appointment to see the town's doctor. When the doctor informed me that I was pregnant with Joshua's baby, it explained my tiredness, mood swings, weight gain, and frequent upset stomach. I'm not sure if I should tell Joshua now or not. I am unsure at this point as to how I feel about having another baby.

Weeks turned into months. I was swamped with homework and a lot of research. I still hadn't told Joshua that I was carrying his baby, but

I knew I needed to. He will be here with the kids in a few weeks for my birthday. I hadn't heard from him in a couple of days, so I decided to call him after my shower to break the news.

I allowed Joshua's phone to ring several times, but he never answered. That's strange, I thought. So, I called Calvin to check in on the boys. The boys were having the time of their lives with Uncle Calvin. I think he was having more fun than them based on his laughter. "Calvin, have you spoken to Joshua lately?" I asked.

"No, Kenna. Come to think of it, he hasn't been by to see the boys either. I will call his dad or go by the house and see what's going on," Calvin said, sounding reassuring.

"Thank you Calvin!" I hung up with him and called to check on Angel. Angel was doing well.

I laid around waiting for a call from Joshua, and still hadn't heard from him. I didn't want to call Calvin back and worry him, but my nerves were getting bad. *Father God, make darkness submit a letter of resignation. Make fear afraid to stand next to me. Amen.*

I had to have faith that things were going to be fine. Joshua will call soon I thought as I dozed off to sleep. I awoke to my phone ringing from a number that I did not recognize. "Hello," I said as I sleepily answered the phone.

"I AM GOING TO KILL YOU BITCH! HE KILLED MY BROTHER AND I AM GOING TO KILL YOU!!" the voice said.

"Huh? Who is this and what are you talking about?" The caller hung up. I was stuck, I had no idea who called or what they were talking about.

I sat on the side of the bed feeling sick to my stomach. Just as I stood to go and relieve my stomach, my phone rang again. "Hello," I answered.

"Hello Kenna, this is Captain St. Clair. I hate to do this but, I need to inform you that Joshua was stabbed several times and left for dead." I couldn't believe my ears! This can't be true!

"Why, who, what happened?" I asked in between tears.

"Marco was released unbeknown to us. He stabbed Joshua multiple times. It was all caught on the church's cameras. Marco approached Joshua taking out the trash. An argument ensued and they began scuffling. Joshua was getting the best of Marco, and that's when Marco pulled out a knife and began stabbing him."

"Joshua is a fighter, and he is still holding on. He has been transported over to General Hospital," Mr. St. Clair continued explaining. "Pastor Benedick is the one who discovered his body. From what he said, Joshua stopped by to talk. On his way out, he volunteered to help take out the trash. When he didn't return, the Pastor went out back looking for him. Joshua's car was still out there, that is what made him go look at the camera's to see which way he went. Joshua's body was discovered behind the church's trash dumpster," he said in between sniffles and a cracked voice."

"Did they find Marco?" I asked.

"No, we haven't but I guarantee you that we will!" he said with heat in his voice.

"I am booking a flight out Mr. St. Clair. I am returning home," I said as I moved around my dorm room packing up my items.

I hurriedly booked a ticket home, called an Uber, and tried mentally preparing myself. I couldn't stop crying or wondering why Marco would go to such extremes. En route to the airport, I called Mr. Singfield and Ms. Agnes to see if they were aware of what was going on. They knew something was going on because the boys were dropped off. They didn't know the details. I filled them in as best I could before having to hang up. I ran through the airport like OJ Simpson in order to check in and make my flight. The lines were extremely long, and security was tight.

I made it! I barely made it, but I made it just in time to board before the doors were closed. I found my seat on the plane and collapsed in my seat. *Father, I am going to embrace this storm. I know it's not here to hurt, but to help me. I also know you have not forsaken me. Please Father, wrap your arms around Joshua. Let your will be the way. In your name Father I pray this, Amen!*

I inserted my earplugs and decided to listen to some Yolanda Adams and relax. Before I knew it, the wheels were up. I awoke to, "Wheels down, thank you for flying Delta." People were standing up and lining up to exit the plane. Finally, I got off of the plane and stood out front awaiting my Uber.

Chapter Thirty-Two

The Bloods Not On My Hands

I called Mr. Singfield to tell him and Agnes to get the kids ready. I was excited to see them, plus I knew as much as they loved them that they would welcome the early pickup. He sounded strange, but I figured that it was me overthinking things. When I arrived, the house was dark. I know they haven't gone to bed or anything, I just spoke to him. I rang the doorbell and Ms. Agnes answered the door. The look on her face told it all. I didn't have to ask any questions. I hurriedly pulled my phone out and called nine one one. I put my phone back in my pocket, put my keys between my fingers and asked God to cover me. I stormed into the house past Ms. Agnes and saw Marco. He was sitting in the living area. Angel was on the couch next to Marco eating noodles. The boys sat on the floor looking too scared to move. Mr. Singfield sat in his chair bruised and beaten.

"Well hello Kenna, you finally arrived. I was getting a little tired of waiting for you to take me seriously. Hmm, looks like you may have been raped again. With child I see!" Marco said sarcastically.

"Angel, come to mommy," I said. Angel put her bowl down and proceeded to get down off of the couch. Marco grabbed her by her arm and told her to sit down, which upset her. "Marco, look, if you want to hurt me, then hurt me! What you are not about to do is harm my children!" I said in response to how he grabbed Angel. That pissed me off.

"Shut up Kenna! You have caused enough damage! Everyone's lives you have encountered have been affected in a negative way! You don't have shit to say to me! I am going to kill you, especially now, Ms. Pregnant! Keep talking and I will show these kids what used to happen at bible study," he said laughingly.

While Marco continued talking, I looked around the room searching for a weapon. I also prayed that the police hurried. I noticed Angel began shaking just like Marco does. I watched as she rocked back and forth. "Get over here," Marco said to me. I took my time walking in his direction. "HURRY UP!" he yelled. I put a little pep in my step and prayed with each step I took. I stood in front of Marco like a kid waiting to be reprimanded. I was not scared of him, I wanted to be careful of my actions so that he would not hurt anyone else further. Every move had to be with precision. Marco reached up and grabbed me by my hair. I fell to the floor sideways with my head halfway on his leg. He pulled with all the strength he had, trying his hardest to rip my hair from my scalp.

"Ouch!" I screamed.

"STOP HURTING MY MOMMY!" Angel cried out.

Before I could say, "NOOO!" Angel took her fork that she ate her noodles with, and stabbed Marco in his eyes. He immediately let go of my hair as he tried getting her off of him and holding his eyes. Blood was everywhere. Mr. Singfield got up and busted him over the head with the lamp. We all jumped on him; the boys included. Ms. Agnes slipped off and got her twenty-two and said," STOP EVERBODY STOP!"

Marco continued screaming. We heard sirens in the distance. I was able to have the boys take Angel and go outside. I tried helping Mr. Singfield and Agnes keep Marco in the house. Marco tried charging Mr. Singfield blindly. Agnes shot him in his back and in his chest. Marco continued to scream and tried getting back up. Ms. Agnes shot him once more in the head before the police came rushing through the front door. Marco looked up at me as I stood and said, "Forgive me," as blood poured from his head. His eyes were hollow and lifeless.

The police questioned Ms. Agnes, Mr. Singfield, and me as the ambulance came in and checked Marco. He was pronounced dead, and the coroner was called. Calvin, and Captain St. Clair came through the door before I was able to breathe a sigh of relief. It is all over, I thought. Captain St. Clair and Calvin comforted Ms. Agnes and Mr. Singfield and assured them that no charges would be filed. After they were able to get everything under control, they spent a few minutes reassuring me, before they both noticed around the same time that I was with child.

"Does Joshua know? Mr. St. Clair asked.

"No, I hadn't had a chance to tell him," I responded.

"Well, it is time that he knows. It will help him to fight harder," Mr. St. Clair said in between smiles.

Ms. Agnes said, "Go on up to that hospital child to see about him."

I walked over to Mr. Singfield and gave him a hug and said," I love you."

Mr. Singfield smiled, and said, "I love you more."

The kids all ran back into the house happy to see Uncle Calvin. He hugged them all as we both explained that I needed to go check on Joshua. They were fine with staying with Ms. Agnes and Mr. Singfield until I returned.

Mr. Singfield allowed me to use his car to run to the hospital. I walked into Joshua's room and was shocked to see that he was connected to several machines. I am not sure why I was so shocked because of the severity of his injuries, but I was.

"Hey Babe," I began, unsure of whether he could hear me or not. "You must keep fighting! I am not going to allow you to give up. It is finally over. Marco is gone, Ms. Agnes shot and killed him. We have a baby coming soon. I did not tell you over the phone because I wanted to wait until you came to see me for my birthday." Joshua turned his head in my direction and tried opening his eyes. He kept putting effort into it until I noticed that he was looking and had a smile on his face. I took his hand and put it on my stomach so that he could feel the life we both created together. I leaned in a little to give him a hug and noticed when I sat back up that he had tears. "Oh, it's okay babe. I am not sure if those are happy tears or not, but I am happy for us." I stayed a while longer before I kissed Joshua and told him that I would be back the next day.

I went back to Mr. Singfield and Ms. Agnes' home to pick the kids up. Mr. Singfield and Ms. Agnes decided that they would drop us off at home. They helped me get the kids' stuff together and put it in the trunk.

I was so grateful for them and Calvin. I am not sure if me surviving all of this would have been possible if God would not have allowed them to play the part that they did in my life.

Once we were home, I had the kids take a shower, then get ready for bed. I sat in my room in thought, and it hit me hard what Angel had done. Angel needs to be assessed; she could have inherited some type of mental illness.

The next day, I went back up to the hospital. Calvin took a vacation day, so he came and picked up the kids. When I walked into the room, Joshua was sitting up looking at the television. "Hey Babe," I said as I entered his room. He forced his head to turn in my direction and had a smile on his face. He struggled but put his own hand on my stomach as he allowed a tear to drop. I sat with him and talked. I fed him and put lotion on his body after the nurse came in and washed him up. I even googled a local barber to have them come up and trim him up.

I sat in a chair next to Joshua as he took a nap. I wanted to be sitting right there when he awoke. I heard a voice in the hall talking and realized that it was Joshua's mom. She gave me a hug and was impressed with how good Joshua looked. We spoke about the baby, and she asked if she could go to my appointment with me until Joshua was healed and could go. I welcomed her to join me. It made me feel good that they were just as excited as I was.

After several weeks, Joshua was released into a nursing facility for therapy. He was progressing well. I made sure that I was there every day and helped in his recovery. After a month or so, he was able to go home.

His therapy continued from there. I visited him at their home, but not as often as I did when he was in the facility. I was getting bigger and lazier. Mrs. St. Clair went with me to my doctors' appointments, and I genuinely enjoyed her company. At my last appointment they did tell me that the baby had turned and was head down. The baby's nursery was set up in Angel's room. Her room was large enough to share for a while.

Time continued flying by. help was an immense help to me. Calvin kept the boys involved in sports, so they stayed busy. Angel enjoyed making cookies and candy with Ms. Agnes and Mr. Singfield. I explained to the kids what was going on with me, and they were excited to add a baby to the mix.

I was not feeling up to myself. After cleaning and doing the laundry, I laid down on the couch and propped my legs up. My back was hurting bad. I Face Timed Joshua to let him know that I may not come by today. It was close to my due date, and I was not feeling well. He and I laughed and talked, although I could tell that he was concerned.

We ended our call, so I decided to take a much-needed nap. It was a great idea until someone began knocking at my door. Oh my GOD, why would anyone stop by without calling, I thought before I got up and opened the door. It was Joshua's sister.

"Hello, I said. How can I help you?"

She looked at me from my head to my feet and said," YOU CAN'T BITCH! I TOLD YOU THAT I WAS GOING TO KILL YOU! POW!!!

My neighbors heard the shots fired and were able to notify the police. The same neighbor that called the police on Charmaine, the Bishop, and the others was the same neighbor that called on Marco's sister. Her exiting her car and walking briskly to my door was recorded on the neighbor's door cam. The door cam also recorded the shots fired and her running back to her car.

My baby was delivered through C-Section and was not harmed, as I lay here in the hospital fighting to live. Her name will be Heavenly if by the grace of God, I make it through this. Fast forward, I have been laying here now for two weeks or so. I know this because Marco tells me what day it is every day.

Marco's family has been bringing him and the baby up to see me. I hate it that I cannot respond to any of them, but I hear them.

Marco's sister was charged with attempted murder, he informed me. Her trial is scheduled for a month from now. Their parents were so furious that they refused to hire an attorney. She must have a court appointed attorney.

My mother came to see me. I heard her faint cries.

"I am so sorry Kenna! I am so sorry that this has happened to you. When I saw it on the news, I almost lost it. I blame myself for not being strong when you needed me the most. It was my responsibility to be your mother, and I failed. The price I am paying for my actions is unbelievable. Yet, I must stand up in it and be accountable. I promise not to leave your side any more until one or we both take our last breath. I also promise to be an exceptional grandmother going forward," my mother cried. I laid there listening to my mother's cries. Instead of feeling sad, I felt at peace. I had forgiven my mother already, she needed to forgive herself.

I had finally awakened. One hundred percent healed. I walked around and embraced the beautiful colors and the peaceful atmosphere. The air smelled clean and refreshing, yet it was all unfamiliar. "Hello, Kenna," he said. I looked and could hardly believe my eyes. It was Marco standing before me. "Marco, I thought you were dead." He smiled before saying," Kenna, I had time to ask and beg for God's forgiveness. He forgave me. Although I died on the other side, God allowed me to be born again with a clean slate.